Between The Mountains

Inspired by a True Dog Story

Jeremy Campbell

The Langston Press

New York City

For Daddy

Life is a matter of perspective.

Contents

Chapter 1: A Dog's Senses 1

Chapter 2: J.D.C. Day 17

Chapter 3: Red Agate and Regret 35

Chapter 4: The Presentation 53

Chapter 5: It's Over 67

Chapter 6: A Banner Year 89

Chapter 7: The Investigation 111

Chapter 8: The Hottest Day 125

Chapter 9: Fourth of July 135

Chapter 10: Hit and Caught 155

Chapter 11: The Recovery 173

Chapter 12: The Cemetery Stroll 189

Chapter 13: Unveiled 209

Chapter 14: Hope 235

Chapter 15: Sacred Harp Songs 255

Chapter 16: Something Borrowed 277

A Message from The Author 291

About the Author 293

CHAPTER 1

A Dog's Senses

Time moves differently for a dog. Scars of the past and worries of the future sit out of mind, like spectators on the riverbank, while a canine's present needs race through his head as fast as water gushes through Morgan's Cove after a summer rain. For the old, black Labrador Retriever lapping a drink from this backwoods stream, the thought of the moment was thirst. Quenching it was his sole focus. His quick, pink tongue sloshed up gulp after gulp and water splashed out of the corners of his gray-fur smile. Crouched beneath the tall pine trees lining the mountain trail, the Lab looked small, although his round belly showed he'd found plenty to eat while making his nomadic rounds. Ivy stretched over the dirt floor of the woods surrounding him, with long green vines winding alongside the water like they were thirsty, too. The dog didn't hear the thump of a red rock that landed hard a few feet away or notice the man who threw it. The white-noise rush of the stream trickled so loudly that a careful predator could easily creep within throwing distance of the dog without being detected. And this one did.

A trio of stones lashed the ground with such force that not even the overgrown ivy softened their impact. This time, the dog heard the thud. His water-dipped smile clenched as his tail stood up at attention; his whiskers pointed outward as the dog's senses heightened. He looked straight ahead, beyond the stream, and locked eyes with a man in a red flannel shirt. Both held their bodies still, in a showdown to discover who would flinch first. The man yanked something out of his pocket, jingled a set of keys attached to his belt, and raised his arm in a fist. He held a near-empty bottle of bourbon in his other hand. The dog lowered his head into submission, slowly stepping backwards as he moved farther away from the stream. His lip snarled, yet the dog's dark eyes shone with the hope that inside the clenched fist was a treat. Bites of beef jerky and sandwich scraps were the usual offerings from humans during the dog's rounds across the mountain.

The man took the last swig from the bottle and dropped it on the ground. He slowly opened his hand, rolling another cold rock across his palm. It was red agate, polished smooth like a gemstone sold at new age stores. Local folks viewed the real value as something more precious than money—many believed red agate protected those who carry it.

This man was throwing stones, not collecting them. His shark-gray eyes tightened in focus and, in one swift move, he lifted the rock, rotated his shoulder, and hurled the red agate at the black Lab.

Whoosh. Ping.

The dog spun around in a half-circle, dodging the impact as he leapt into a full-on sprint through the woods. His hind legs galloped as he maneuvered his body around fallen trees and thick overgrowth much too dense for a human to navigate on foot. He ran and ran and ran until, just as quickly as he started his escape, the old Lab stopped. He chose a spot beneath a magnolia tree covered in summer blossoms. The Lab crouched under its wide branches to catch his breath and, with the man out of sight, danger drifted out of his mind. Back in the peaceful present, the aroma of the blossoms, even more profound to a dog's keen senses, offered a short-lived reprieve for the black Lab. Before his panting could subside, a new sound whirred in the distance. The rev of an engine grew louder and louder until the dog saw the source of the noise spinning from the other direction as it shredded through the underbrush. The man in red flannel drove his four-wheeler straight toward him.

Crack. Snap. Whoosh.

The man sped through the woods, his belt-loop keys jangling with every bump as his pace increased. This time, the Lab tried a different escape plan, trotting mid-speed just fast enough to stay about thirty yards ahead of the four-wheeler. He was smart, as though he had played this game before. The dog seemed to understand that the rocky terrain of the mountainside made it impossible for the human to throttle up too quickly. His animal adaptability allowed for pivots over and under and between wooded spaces much too cumbersome for a six-foot-tall man. The chase continued until the two adversaries approached Langston Gap Road.

Thud. Thump.

A chunk of red agate bounced off the tree ahead of the dog. Just a stone's throw away from one another, he risked running out of forest before crossing into the twisty, asphalt double-lane of Langston Gap Road. The dog's escape tactics wouldn't work there, without the cover of fallen trees and twisted vines.

Thump. Crack. Thud.

The red rocks peppered the air like hail and the dog tucked his tail between his legs. He looked back—the man in red flannel was only a few feet behind him. That's when the first stone hit the dog just between his eyes. In quick succession, a second rock stung his rear left leg, then a third bounced off his back. His old body jolted and twisted with each impact, as his eyes widened in both pain and confusion.

"I've got you," the man yelled, his keys jangling like an alarm on his belt loop warning that time was up.

They were just a few feet from the roadway when a vehicle appeared on Langston Gap Road. The Lab looked at the oncoming car then glanced back at the four-wheeler and picked up his pace. He ran faster and faster toward the speeding car, ignoring the pain in his leg where the rock pelted him. The man in red flannel gripped hard on the handle to crank the gas up all the way.

Whirrrrrrrr.

The engine roared as their chase evolved into a game of chicken, the four-wheeler gaining on the Lab while he galloped straight toward the car. As the ivy-dappled ground turned to pebbly pavement beneath the tires of the four-wheeler, the black Lab leapt forward, lunging just past the car's bumper and landing safely on the other side of the road. The four-wheeler spun out in a double circle as the man in red flannel whipped the wheels away from the road and slid to a stop in a thicket of briars.

In the backseat of the passing car, Arley Flores looked up from her phone for the first time in an hour. Instead of enjoying the scenery during the ride from the airport, she'd obsessively stared at her screen, waiting for a text message to appear. The commotion outside was a welcome distraction from her anxieties about returning to her Alabama hometown after nine months away at college.

"Did you see that?" The driver asked, his voice heaving from the adrenaline rush of a near miss. "That dog came out of the woods like it was running for its life!"

Arley tucked her long brown hair over her shoulder, then squeezed the two-studded aqua earrings she wore in her right ear, as she often did when she was anxious. As she leaned forward to answer her driver, the sunlight sparkled on her gilded rings and the colorful thrift store jewelry wrapped around her neck and wrists. Arley's champagne tastes came to life at second-hand stores, and her daily wardrobe showcased all of her frugal treasures. Every inch of her body seemed adorned in woven bracelets, beaded braids, or shiny things. Even the black linen jumpsuit that swallowed her petite frame had a frayed trim that seemed to tickle her olive skin. The driver barely gave Arley a breath to speak before he pulled over and sprang out of the car, leaving his paying passenger alone in the backseat. His priority appeared to be helping the man in red flannel, who stood perfectly safe on the roadside about half a football field behind him.

"Hey, sir! You ok? That your dog?"

The man raised his arm. This time, his hand opened in a wave, without a rock clenched in his fist. He grinned at the driver and shrugged, fidgeting with the jangling keys attached to his belt loop.

"I hope I didn't scare away your dog," the driver said. "Need me to help you find him?"

The driver watched the man climb back on the four-wheeler, crank it up, and ride away into the woods without saying a word.

"Guess he didn't hear me," he said to Arley.

"Yeah, sure," she said, skeptical of the entire scene. She stood outside of the car now, her vegan leather backpack slung over her shoulder and a giant yellow duffel bag balanced on her hip.

"Where are you going? You're not canceling the ride, are you? I know things got bumpy, but it was the dog, not my driving."

"You're good. Five stars. I'll leave them now. I just feel like walking the rest of the way. It's not that far," she lied, as she tried to conceal her desire to be alone.

"Are you sure? I don't do many drop-offs this far out—seems kind of isolated."

"It's home to me here," she said. That wasn't a lie. "It'll be good for me to clear my head."

"As long as you don't ding my driver rating—"

Arley let out a deep sigh as she pulled up her phone, which was still silent with no replies to all the texts she'd sent to her mom after her flight landed. And there was no response to any of her calls, either. Arley had left a voicemail from baggage claim, then left several more as she waited for her mother to pick her up as planned.

Arley opened the rideshare app and gave her driver a five-star review, plus a tip she couldn't really afford. Paying for a ride home to Jackson County from the Huntsville airport is not common, if it's done at all between the mountains. The drive is too far, and the neighborhoods are too rural for drivers to find their next customer, but Arley didn't know who else to call, even if it meant spending all the money she thought she'd use on a summer pass to the pool at the community center.

"Thanks for the tip, and good luck on your walk. If you see that man's dog maybe you can help connect them," the driver said.

"You realize that dog was running away from that man, right? He isn't the owner."

"How do you know that?"

"Because he drove off on the wrong side of the road. The dog crossed over the other way. No dog owner would head in the opposite direction of their pet. They'd go find it."

"Hmmm...I guess so."

Ding. Buzz. Beep.

An alert on his cell phone confirmed she'd left the driver five stars as promised. That was enough to send him on his way, leaving the young woman alone on the two-lane backroad.

Arley began her walk home. She had about half a mile ahead of her, but it felt much longer. Her clunky black boots crunched the gravel on the road's shoulder as she stared up at sunlight filtering through the tall pine trees. A breeze swirled down the edge of the mountain ridge behind her as she followed the two-lane road past hay fields and old wooden barns. Arley used to wander these roads every summer as a child to fill time. This May marked nearly ten months since she last traveled down them to leave home for college in Texas. With each step closer, her anxiety intensified about returning after so many months away. It was about more than the distance apart. She was far from who she'd once been, too. During her freshman year at college, she grew; thanks to new experiences with new friends with different interests, and a few college crushes. In Austin, the uncertainty of fresh experiences excited the small-town girl. Here, everything seemed the same, and Arley felt nervous about what everyone would think of her if they realized how much she'd changed.

Arley neared a neighbor's rusty fence, a sign that she was almost home. Her beaded bracelets and eccentric rings suddenly made her feel more self-conscious than self-confident. She scanned the pasture, looking for the herd of buffalo it usually contained—as a child, she'd spent many hours marveling at the majestic animals. As quickly as she wondered what happened to all the buffalo, she found the herd hiding from the sun under the shade of a tree—together.

The sight spurred a theory that eased her anxiety: *My mom didn't return my texts or calls because she's planning a surprise party to welcome me home.* After all, Arley had messaged her just before takeoff at Hobby Airport, then sent an *"Almost home"* text during her layover in Atlanta, and left several voicemails after she landed in Huntsville. The only logical explanation for the radio silence had to be because her mom was busy preparing the balloons and streamers, and telling guests where to hide before belting out *"Surprise!"* Hope ran deep in Arley.

She quickened her pace and her heart pounded as she swigged in fast breaths of honeysuckle-scented country air along the roadside. Her bright yellow duffel bag grew cumbersome in her arms. She carried it like an overgrown dog that's too large to be held and the strap on the duffel rubbed against her shoulder, pressing on a metal pin fastened to the handle. The pressure pinched its hard edges into her skin, and Arley grimaced at the small metal flag causing so much pain. Its rainbow stripes irritated her with every step on her walk home. She decided to remove the pin, hiding it away inside the front pocket of her bag.

"*Everything will be okay this summer,*" she told herself, wondering if she should remove some of her colorful jewelry, too.

The landscape changed the closer Arley got to her parents' house. On the ride up Langston Gap Road, she had anxiously stared out of the backseat window at the steep, hold-on-to-your-heart highway. About two feet made all the difference between a beautiful view and an off-the-cliff tragedy. Her pulse raced then, but it beat even faster after she arrived in her old neighborhood. On this side of the mountain, sweeping cattle fields surrounded ranch-style homes. That's where Arley found herself, just as the charge in her headphones went dead. In the silence, she arrived at the second split-level on the right, and it looked exactly as she remembered it. Outside, the driveway sat empty with no cars in the garage, no vehicles lining the street and no signs of any guests from the party waiting to yell "*Surprise!*"

Clink. Clink. Thud.

Arley turned the front door handle, but the deadbolt blocked her from entering. Her shoulder ached and she dropped the yellow duffel bag to the ground as she sent another text to her mom, *"Are you ok? I just got home. Where are you?"*

She ran her hand over the door ledge and, just like old times, she found a spare key hanging over the entryway. Inside, the air smelled familiar, fresh like fabric softener and sweet like the chocolate chip cookies her dad baked on Saturdays. She kept the lights off as she wandered through the rooms of her past, examining each with both nostalgia and hope that someone would be there to surprise her. She checked her bedroom, now converted into her mom's home gym, before exploring the black and white tile-floored kitchen, then her parents' room with the giant yellow bed, and finally the sunken living room. It was always her favorite because of the light green wall-to-wall carpet and the tiny bay window that offered just enough of a wooden edge for Arley to act out plays or to sing *"On Top of Spaghetti"* for imaginary audiences.

Arley sat on the soft satin-lined couch in the center of the room, wondering where everyone had gone, when she heard a rustle coming from the other side of the piano. Her eyes widened and her heart raced as she ran over to look behind the bench. Instead of her family, she discovered a little gray bunny in a cage, trembling with fear.

"*I guess people do change,*" Arley thought, remembering all those years she'd begged her mother for a pet only to be told they make too much of a mess. This little rabbit couldn't make any messes caged up in the corner. She smiled at the bunny and unlatched the metal door, holding out her palm.

"It's ok, I'm a friend. I guess I'm technically your sister," she laughed. "You're free!"

The bunny's dark, wide eyes stared up at Arley as it hopped toward her, sniffing the colorful beaded bracelet dangling beneath her wrist. She scooped the warm bunny in her arms and gently ran her index finger between its eyes and down the back of its head, feeling the rabbit's heart rate settle as it realized she was a friendly human. Arley's anxiety seemed to fade, too, as she found solace with the bunny.

"Guess it's just me and you, sis. I promise I'll be back for you," Arley said, as she returned the bunny to its cage and looked out the bay windows. Outside, she noticed an old, black Lab sitting on his hind legs beneath the willow tree in her front yard. He seemed to peer into the house, smiling at her.

"*Don't tell me they got a dog, too,*" she thought, as she walked up to the glass to get a better look. But this dog didn't appear to belong to anyone. No collar, no tag—just a pink, slobbery smile. He looked exactly like the dog she'd seen bolting across Langston Gap Road, except now he was sprawled on the grass, relaxed and confident. His big, brown eyes seemed familiar, like an old friend she hadn't met yet. From the front porch, Arley called out, *"Hey, boy!"* He stood, wagged his tail, and trotted over to her with a steady and deliberate pace, pressing his head against her leg before thumping down on the stoop beside her.

Ding. Buzz. Ding.

As she sat on the front step beside him, Arley's cell phone lit up with incoming text messages arriving all at once.

Mom: Hi, honey! We're ok. Your dad and I are at the airport hotel. There was a reception here for one of my coworkers. We meant to just stop for just a minute, but I lost track of time and forgot about your flight. Oops!

Dad: Sorry honey! You know where the key is, right?

Mom: Maybe you can unpack while you wait for us? Your clothes must be a pile of wrinkles if you're still traveling with that old duffel bag!

Arley shrugged her shoulders and tightly closed her eyes, trying to ignore the emotions that welled up inside her. Even if she trapped those feelings under a boulder on Langston Gap Road, that pressure wouldn't have been enough to keep tears from smudging her dark eyeliner. Being forgotten felt bad enough, but Arley felt embarrassed for having thought, even for a moment, that her parents' lack of communication was an act of consideration. The only surprise here was that her homecoming celebration was a party of one.

As Arley wiped away teardrops, she felt a tickle on her cheek. It was the old, black Lab, gently licking away her salty tears and smudged make-up. He placed his head in her lap and sighed. Like the bunny had before him, the dog unexpectedly soothed Arley. Animals were new to her, never having cared for a pet of her own, but she liked how this felt. As her thoughts caught up with her emotions, the lab pulled himself up from her lap, pranced down the front steps, and began walking across the field outside her home. He moved toward the path she used to take to the community center where she worked during summer break. She wanted out of the empty house, and the community center seemed like a good place for her to go. Maybe the dog would come along, too.

"Wait up, old boy!"

Arley quickly scribbled out a note to her parents, explaining where she was going, then locked up. She chased the Lab through the field of knee-high grass, never once looking back at the empty house behind her.

CHAPTER 2

J.D.C. Day

"Okay, everybody, it's almost time. Places!"

Patty Wylde didn't measure time by minutes as much by moments, and she had a knack for predicting just when the timing was right. She learned to feel the rhythm of North Star Community Center beginning a few decades ago when she was in her twenties working as a registration assistant. She snapped countless photos for ID badges and organized membership drives, knowing a bigger moment would arrive for her...and it did. Her promotion to office manager partnered her with J.D. Campbell, who Patty predicted would run the place one day. And again, the moment arrived. With J.D. at the helm as director of the center, Patty played defense to his quarterback, filtering out distractions and reminding the team what they're all working toward. But on Wednesday afternoons, her job became a party.

"Today's J.D.C. Day celebration begins when J.D.'s five o'clock meeting ends, which should be in about three minutes," Patty told the room.

"But that meeting usually lasts until six," Jana said.

"In three minutes. Trust me."

After so many years at the community center with J.D., Patty kept the schedule on track by paying attention to small things like a raised eyebrow, the tone of a voice, or how fast J.D.'s knee bounced. She read the tells like a second language.

"Brenda, put the gumbo on the table with the deviled eggs. Trish, turn off the lights," Patty said. "It's time."

She kept the festivities moving on schedule as co-workers raced into the lobby of the Director's Office for their weekly Wednesday faux surprise. Part of the charm was to pretend it was all unexpected, as if a dozen people just happened to cram in the lobby together with a potluck dinner spread out across the office. Brenda protected the gumbo with care, as they all waited with the lights off for the cue to celebrate. The one thing they forgot was to be quiet.

"Shhhh! He won't come out if he hears us out here starting without him!" Patty warned.

Just as she expected, exactly three minutes later, J.D.'s door opened into the dark room. He'd removed his blazer and unbuttoned his shirt collar for the first time since before breakfast. When his sleeves were rolled up, his workday was done. J.D. stepped into the lobby with an ever-so-slight smile on his face and said the magic words that started the celebration every week.

"I guess it's quittin' time," he shrugged, as though having the lights off concealed his coworkers.

He heard a couple of whispered giggles spread across the stillness of the lobby and cleared his throat to speak louder this time, his tone exaggerated.

"Well, I guess it must be quittin' time!"

And with that, Trish pressed a button on her smartphone to power on blue and green party lights that swirled around the office. In unison, Brenda pushed play on the New Orleans music playlist programmed into her phone as Patty and the team cheered three words that kicked off the after-work celebration: *"Happy J.D.C. Day!"*

At offices across the country it was just another Wednesday, but at North Star Community Center, mid-week was reason enough to celebrate. There always seemed to be a new achievement worth heralding. This week alone, J.D. cut the ribbon on a new softball field, recruited two new volunteers, and planned how to make the annual Latino Festival even bigger than last year.

Outside the party, looking through the glass door of the lobby, Arley watched the crowd pass around bowls of gumbo and hunks of sliced bread from the Mennonite market down the road. She knew exactly what they were celebrating from her high school summers when she worked at reception in the Director's Office. With her long hair twirling around her index finger, a tug-of-war unfolded in her mind. She wanted to go inside to connect with everyone but, after her unceremonious welcome at her parents' house, she lacked the confidence to arrive uninvited. Her mind raced with reasons they wouldn't accept her, from the extra piercings in her ears to the fact that she hadn't been in touch since she left for college. After almost a year away, she wasn't sure if she'd still fit in at the community center.

"How can I just waltz into J.D.C. Day after going M.I.A. for so long?" she wondered.

As she tugged at the belt on her jumpsuit, Arley's own reflection caught her focus in the mirror across the hall—the same framed mirror she once used to check the progress of her teeth aligners and fuss with her hair. The worried young woman in the reflection looked unrecognizable compared to the girl who used to smile back. As the flashing, multicolored lights from the J.D.C. Day celebration illuminated her clenched brow, she imagined her mother's voice, "*Imperfect posture is the calling card of imperfect people.*" Arley straightened her spine and pulled back her slumped shoulders. Her mother taught her how you look is more important than how you feel.

Something darted by in the mirror's reflection. She peered into the lobby and saw the old, black Lab she'd followed from her parent's house. Not only had they ended up at the same destination, but the dog had somehow made it inside the community. "*How?!*" Arley wondered. She watched as the dog greeted each person in the room just like J.D. did, almost as though the human and canine operated in tandem. When the Lab sensed Arley watching, he barked loudly at the glass door separating her from the party. She found herself the center of attention with all eyes looking at her. In a beat, Patty opened the door and pulled her inside.

"As I live and breathe, Arley Flores!" Patty smiled. "Get in here, girl! This party just got cranked up a notch now that you're joining us!"

Patty hugged her with a squeeze so tight it forced her tense shoulders down and her arms open. It wasn't the grip that forced Arley to relax—it was the love.

"We have a homecoming celebration on our hands! It's been too long, and we've all missed you so much!"

From the vice grip of the embrace, Arley noticed the black Lab slowly turned around, as though he'd completed his job by herding her into the room. He swaggered back outside, walking through the long, orange shadows cast by the summer sunset. The Lab glimmered in the top-of-the-mountain glow as he ambled out of sight. She wondered, "*Where is he off to next?*" However, there wasn't much time to think about that as the room seemed to revolve around her, with former colleagues from the community center asking about her year at college. Each person greeted her with a small plate from the J.D.C. Day buffet, filling her stomach with gumbo, macaroni and cheese, and even a slice of cake from the bakeshop in the town square. J.D.'s wife, Bell, sent over a white buttercream decorated with blue flowers, specially prepared for the group every Wednesday.

As the satisfying sluggishness of a food coma settled in, Arley walked down the long, narrow hallway to J.D.'s office. She may as well have walked back through time. Arley marveled at the mementos from J.D.'s storied life, including the framed concert posters of the many famous musicians who played at the community center back when they were hopeful unknowns, before they became titans of bluegrass and roots rock. J.D. recognized greatness even when he was an unknown himself, at grad school in Austin forty years ago. Like Arley, he was a Long Horn. Degrees from Scottsboro High School, Auburn University, Florida State, and the University of Texas lined the wall alongside his collection of art, featuring scenes from Louisiana to New Mexico. She noticed gold pens from legislation signed into law, a tile salvaged from a remodel at the United States Capitol, and shovels J.D. used for groundbreaking ceremonies throughout two counties. Trophies and plaques lined every spare space of his office. The community center and its many volunteers seemed to have been honored with every triumph and tribute under the sun.

"J.D. is like the gold setting to the Hope Diamond," Arley whispered, "He knows how to make people shine."

On the corner of his desk, she saw framed photos of his mother from decades ago and several of his wife, Bell, taken across the decades, plus snapshots of some coworkers like Trish and Patty who'd become more like family. In a small brass square frame, she spotted a photo of a little brown dog at the vet clinic off Langston Road. J.D. and his wife Bell stood next to the pup named Poppy, posed in front of a mural at the clinic as yellow butterflies swirled around them.

"That's Poppy!" Arley exclaimed, unaware J.D. had walked up beside her.

"Yes, it is. That little dog captivated the entire town," he said.

"I didn't see you there!"

"I've been trying to say hello all night but you're the guest of honor. Every time I got close, someone else commandeered you."

"They would have stepped aside for you," Arley said, nervously staring at the photographs on the wall. "I hope you don't mind that I was looking at your pictures."

"That's what they're here for!"

Staring at one photo more closely than the others, J.D. squinted to focus. Reviewing budget proposals and development plans all day left his dark brown eyes tired, but the kindness never drooped from them. His face was naturally tan, even when his long workdays often kept him out of the sun, and his skin had a golden hue to it that drew people in. He pointed to the picture of the little brown dog. "So, you know about Poppy?"

"Well, I know of her. I was part of the group text chain a few years ago. I read all about how your wife and her friends rescued Poppy off the side of Langston Road."

"That's a while back, but people still talk about how that little dog brought the town together," J.D. smiled. "Funny how dogs can do that. They are the best of us."

"You know, a dog actually led me here today. Did you see that black Lab that was in the office when I arrived?"

"Oh, you mean ol' Roscoe? He's our nomad. Roscoe roams all over, but he's practically moved in here," J.D. said as a stroke of pride washed over his face. He pulled his shoulders back and smoothed his salt-and-pepper hair. Just thinking of the dog made him stand a little taller.

"Moved in? Like, your office?"

"My office. The lobby. The cafeteria. He takes naps in the computer center. Sometimes, if it's nice outside, he even hangs around in the dugout at the new softball field. He's a free spirit, but his home is here at the community center," J.D. explained. "Roscoe chose us."

"Roscoe—I like that name!"

Thump. Thump. Thump. Whoosh!

In a runaway rumble, young Anna interrupted their conversation like a thunderclap. She ran down the hallway with heavy stomps, and the streamer she'd been twirling at the J.D.C. Day celebration was tied into her curly blonde hair. The child's usual rosy cheeks burned fiery red as she screamed out to J.D.

"She's lost her mind, Mr. J.D.! Can you…just…do…something?!" Anna's frustration impeded her from finding the words to explain what happened. "Fire her! You've got to fire my grandmama!"

J.D. played along.

"Anna, we've gotten no personnel complaints about Patty, but I take these types of issues seriously. It's my belief that all conflicts have two sides to the story: One that's obvious and another side that may not be as easy to see. Life is a matter of perception. Would you like to file an official report about your grandmama?"

"Yes! Take notes!" Anna commanded.

"I'll need to hear her side, too."

"Oh, this conflict only has one side to it!"

Anna settled into the tall, leather-studded chair in front of J.D.'s oak desk, which was covered with an assortment of to-do lists, contracts, and newspapers held down with seemingly ordinary paperweights. Upon closer look, these knickknacks were actually awards, including a key to the city of his hometown and a citizen of the year award from the DeKalb County Commission. J.D. pulled out a yellow steno pad and a pen from beneath the pile, then slipped on his reading glasses for dramatic effect.

"So, what seems to be the problem, Anna?"

"Well, you're looking right at it, Mr. J.D. See my hair?!" Anna said, holding up a knotted blonde braid laced with a colorful streamer. "Cousin Lilah tied my hair in knots with that party decoration!"

"It looks very festive. But if you don't like it, I'm sure your grandmama will help you take it out."

"Oh, I can cut it out if I need to," Anna said, her blue eyes bulging. "But my grandmama told me that Lilah and I had to sort it out on our own."

"Ok, well, that doesn't sound so bad."

"No, it's her job to sort things like this out! But that's not why I think you should fire her. That part is coming up, are you writing all of this down in your report?" she asked. "I told Grandmama Patty I'd rather fight Lilah than sort it out with her."

"We don't allow fighting around here, Anna."

"This is the part where my grandmama lost it!"

"Are you telling on me, Anna?" Patty asked as she walked in the room, scooped the child into her lap and began untangling. Patty tossed her own hair over her shoulder. It curled like Anna's, but her own golden highlights had turned into grey streaks after forty. She wore them like a badge of honor. Her well-coordinated outfits dared anyone to see her as anything but stylish, even dressed in a practical heel.

"Look, all I did was establish the rules for your fight club. It was you who wanted to duke it out with your cousin," said Patty.

She explained that the spirited grandkids bicker from time to time, which wasn't news to J.D. Patty shared her perspective, describing how after the crowd from the J.D.C. Day celebration cleared out, Patty took the girls to the lobby to settle their disagreement. Rather than avoiding conflict, Patty believed in establishing ground rules for a fair fight— at least that's what she told the girls.

"Before the fight begins, what rules do you want for your fight club?" Patty asked.

"Rules?" Anna questioned.

"Yeah, rules. Like, do you want to allow everything?"

"Yes! No rules! No rules!" Lilah cheered.

"Well, okay. I guess I'll have to get some ointment from the first aid kit."

"Ointment?!" Anna scoffed.

"Yeah, if you allow anything that includes biting, which could lead to an infection. Have you seen your cousin's sharp teeth?"

"Maybe we should add in a rule for no biting," Lilah said.

"So, no biting, but anything else goes?" Patty asked. "Even hair pulling?"

"That's what got us into this in the first place!" Anna yelled.

"Okay, okay. No biting. No hair pulling. What about a slap?"

"Well...that might leave a mark," Anna worried.

Ultimately, after hearing a half dozen hypothetical methods of warfare, they decided not to fight, which had been Patty's goal all along—but Anna wanted her reprimanded for suggesting it.

"You see the problem, J.D., is that my granddaughters want me to do their dirty work," Patty said, as she pulled the streamer from Anna's hair.

"Can you believe she was trying to start a fight club?!" Anna whispered to J.D. "She's lost her mind!"

"Well, thank you for submitting this report, Anna." said J.D. "I'll review the case, but, before I decide on disciplinary action, I must ask you one thing. Your grandmother just untangled that knot from your hair, which seemed to start the fight. Don't you think maybe that's worth a pardon this time?"

"Ahh!" Anna gasped, as her small fingers ran through her golden hair, realizing the streamer untangled and her curls were intact. She'd been so focused on telling the story, she didn't notice Patty gently removed the tangle.

"Thanks, Grandmama!" she said after she gave Patty a quick kiss on the cheek and ran back to the lobby to find Lilah.

"Do I need to update my resume, J.D.?" Patty laughed. "Am I a retiree again?"

"I think we all need to be on our best behavior around Anna. She's the real boss around here—and she's not afraid to fire us all!"

"I was ready to update my resume...and I don't even work here anymore!" Arley joked. She appeared relaxed and hadn't looked at her text messages since arriving at the community center.

"You know I don't work here anymore either," Patty said, her eyes gleaming.

"What?" Arley said.

"Nope, I'm retired!"

"And re-hired," J.D. added.

"Newly retired and newly rehired," Patty explained.

Exactly one month after her retirement party, Patty showed up incognito in J.D.'s office with a fake resume. She wore a hat as big as an Easter bonnet, with dark glasses and a silk scarf around her neck, but J.D. didn't miss a beat. Even in that get-up, he put her through his usual get-to-know you, which included the tough interview questions. Never once did either of them break character. The act continued until J.D. invited her to accept a part-time consulting role and she said, *"Heck yes!"* on the spot.

After the handshake Patty had asked, "How did my fake name get through your background check?" J.D. confessed he figured out the charade from what she wrote in her cover letter. Patty had included a top ten list of reasons she'd be perfect for the role, and they were all custom J.D.-isms, from *"never whine"* to *"knowing when to shut up."* At the number one spot, she swore never to be negative. Instead, she promised, *"If there's a way we can do it, it will be done!"*

"That's how I knew it was her," J.D. explained to Arley. "Even in camouflage, I recognized Patty's personality."

"Hard for me to hide it!" she said. "I suppose Anna inherited that from me."

"Why did you want to come back so soon?" Arley asked.

"Oh, I thought J.D. needed me around to remind him when it's time to take a break. He works too hard."

Thump. Thump. Thump. Thump.

Anna ran back to the office, this time with Lilah two steps behind her. Both of their faces were dripping with tears, as Lilah slid herself up on Patty's lap and Anna grabbed J.D.'s arm, pulling it around her for protection. They appeared both terrified and heartbroken.

"Something is wrong with Roscoe," Anna blurted out. "He's bleeding red all over the carpet."

They all rushed to the lobby where they found the old Lab in the center of the room, smiling as wide as ever. It was his usual glad-to-see-you expression, even though his body bent to the side as though he could not find a comfortable place to settle. A small trail of blood dripped behind him. J.D. rushed to his side as Arley followed the red blotted tracks back out through the glass door.

"Are you ok, ol' boy? What happened to you?"

He discovered a small puncture on his rear leg, no bigger than the tip of a pen. It was oozing blood. J.D. rubbed his hand around the bone near Roscoe's foot and felt upwards toward the dog's back hips. Roscoe tensed his muscles and the smile vanished from his face. The dog was in pain. Arley raced back inside, her chest heaving as she tried to catch her breath. She held up a handful of rocks; they were a deep red color and shaped more like polished gemstones than pieces of granite.

"I followed the drips of blood all the way to the empty parking lot behind the student center. These rocks were scattered all around there. I thought it seemed...odd," Arley explained. Her heart raced as she saw J.D. lying face-to-face with Roscoe. "Is he going to be okay?"

"Let's get him to the vet clinic. Patty, can you call Emma and Charles and let them know we are on the way?"

"I already texted them, J.D. And I sent a picture of Roscoe's wound."

"But it's after hours," Arley said. "No vet clinic will be open after six."

"Emma and Charles will open for Roscoe. Want to ride with us? You can finally meet Poppy. She lives at the clinic," he said.

Arley had become obsessed with Poppy summers ago, when she first worked at the community center. She would overhear J.D. giving updates about his wife's quest to rescue the little dog from the side of Langston Road. To stay up to date, Arley joined a text group chain about Emma, Charles, and Bell's efforts. When word spread that they'd finally saved the dog after a full year of trying, Arley felt so invested in the animal that it was almost as though she'd been along for the rescue herself. She was excited at the prospect of meeting the dog in real life, but as she looked at the clock across the room, she wondered if her parents were home yet. Then she remembered the empty house, and how alone she'd felt until she saw Roscoe. Now it was her chance to be there for him.

"I'd love to go with you," she said. "Let's get Roscoe to the vet!"

In the lobby of North Star Community Center, Roscoe stared at J.D. with soulful, helpless eyes. He lifted the heavy dog and began carrying him to his car. The Lab rested his head on his person's shoulder as the J.D.C. Day celebration ended unlike any other—with an emergency transport to the vet.

CHAPTER 3

<hr>

Red Agate and Regret

"**E**mma Hodges. Now *that* is a name!" Charles said.

His smile beamed so brightly that it deflected the daggers shooting from Emma Johnson's squinted, brown eyes.

"I think Hodges is the perfect last name for you, Emma. It's served me well for thirty-nine years!"

Emma clawed her cherry-painted fingernails at him but her hand only grabbed a fistful of air. She practically growled at Charles Hodges to step back.

"Hodges? That's *your* name, Charles." Emma's slow Southern accent dragged the word "your" across the floor and plopped it in his face. "Why would I want to take someone else's name, anyway? That's what got me into this predicament in the first place!"

She covered her left hand, hiding her bare ring finger out of habit. More than a decade had passed since she threw her wedding band off the B. B.

Comer Bridge and watched it sink into the depths of the Tennessee River, which was her way of burying the hatchet. Even after all these years, whenever the subject of her last name came up, her right hand covered her left.

"I don't think you get it," she said.

Charles leaned back in the chair behind the reception desk at the clinic, his crisp veterinarian's coat open over a green-and-black checkered shirt. Since he and Emma opened their animal clinic together, he'd learned *"I don't think you get it"* translated to *"I'm about to tell you something."*

Emma pushed up the baggy cuffs of her denim shirt, hands positioned on her hips, her shirt collar popped up just enough so her spiral braids bounced over the trim. At five foot four, Emma had a way of standing taller than anyone in the room. Her power pose was augmented by reflections from a galaxy of light emanating from a sparkly glass case in the lobby's corner. It was her artistic showcase, a gemstone store that she alone owned. Emma agreed to go into business with Charles only after negotiating her own corner of independence. Since only he was licensed to treat animals, she needed something solely for herself, even if it required an extra form on Tax Day.

Her business license was of the self-taught variety. She gained experience from her many entrepreneurial attempts, always earning just enough to support herself and then, after her ex left her with a toddler, earning enough to support her child, too. When the ex had walked out years ago, she'd doubled down on always maintaining self-sufficiency, even if it meant wearing a last name that belonged to someone else. Johnson was his name, but it belonged to Sia, too.

"For seventeen unlucky years I've worn this name like a life sentence. I thought I had to because I share it with my child."

Charles nodded, his eyes glancing at the framed photo of Sia and her mother. It hung between the bejeweled dog leashes and crystal-studded dog collars Emma sold in her corner shop. The snapshot showed the pair standing by the pine trees off the side of Langston Road, smiles as wide as the river. Poppy, the famously stray pup, stood a few feet behind them. Emma and Charles had spent a year trying to rescue the little brown dog from the side of the dangerous road. They'd text updates to J.D.'s wife, Bell, who felt an ache to do right by the helpless animal. The strangers joined forces when they realized they had all been leaving food out for the stray between the causeways on Langston Road. The photo on the wall represented more than a rescue. It documented a beginning for the three friends, and for Charles and Emma, the potential for so much more. In the photo, Charles noticed how different Sia looked now. At the time, Sia was a pre-teen who had to be driven to school every day. They'd speed along the twists and turns of Langston Road in Emma's Jeep, keeping a lookout for Poppy. Now, Sia was behind the wheel of that old Jeep. Poppy lived with Charles and, when their clinic became a success after all the attention from Poppy's rescue, Emma was able to afford a new Prius. Through all that, Emma still carried the same last name of a man who'd left her feeling anything but successful.

"Can you imagine, Charles—seventeen years? That's thousands of times I've introduced myself with his name. When it escapes my lips, the word *Johnson* feels like a regret being forced out of me. I kept it for Sia—and it turns out, my child couldn't care less!"

Emma turned her back to Charles. He knew her well enough to tell this was a signal that she was about to reveal something. He leaned forward with his lips slightly curled upward in a smile of support. Charles' boyish expressions and fair skin made him look younger than he really was. He'd turn forty next year, just a couple years ahead of Emma. As he watched her shoulders heave up, she took a deep breath in and reached for one of the smooth gemstones from a sales bin marked "courage" on the glass countertop of her booth. He leaned forward with a slight smile on his face, curious what she may say next. Charles hung on her every word, endlessly fascinated by Emma, especially when she was being dramatic.

"For seventeen unlucky years I've written this name like I was exposing a shameful tattoo—"

"Written?" Charles interrupted. "Where? On checks? Are you still doing that, Emma? I thought we got you set up on autopay."

"It's a metaphor, Charles."

"And I must be honest, Emma. I think that frog tattoo on your foot is nothing to be ashamed of. It's actually kind of cute."

He knew how to pester Emma from an eight all the way up to an eleven on her "annoyed scale."

"My point is," Emma said, stretching the "s" out like she was talking in cursive. "Sia told me it doesn't matter if we have the same last name, as long as I get their pronouns right. It was an ah-ha moment for me. Here, I've been holding on to this badge of shame, like I'm some kind of martyr...and the jokes on me, Charles—nobody cares!"

"I think you should change it. Free yourself, Emma. Change your name!"

Emma sighed with relief, signifying that she felt heard and understood. She quickly kissed the orange courage-emitting gemstone, unclenched her fist, and released it back into the sales bin. Charles' support had a way of cooling boiling water just before it bubbled over the sides of her pot.

"A name change is so expensive, though. You wouldn't believe all you have to go through."

"That's my point, Emma. If you get married, it's not as complicated. Or as expensive."

"First of all, I don't need some man riding in on a horse to save me. And second of all, if this *is* a marriage proposal, I'm calling HR. We're business partners! This is inappropriate!"

She stood up and smoothed down the collars of her shirt as she smiled nervously, her deep red lipstick contrasting with her brown complexion.

"This is a business proposal, Emma. Marry me. Change your name. Then we'll have it annulled. The name can stick. Easy and affordable."

"I hadn't thought of it like that," she said. "That might work. But you'd do that for me?"

"I'd do anything for you," his eyes locked with hers, his face serious as stone. "But you'll need HR approval."

"Oh, yes." Her eyes fluttered as she looked down at the ground, as though she were in trouble at work. "Do you think HR will approve it?"

"Emma! You are HR!"

They laughed deeply, so joyous that Poppy popped through the kennel door into the lobby to see what happened. The brown Mountain Cur from Langston Road had grown thicker, healthier, and confident. Her ears perked up as she gazed at her keepers, then Poppy's focus shifted to the front door. Dogs hear something coming long before people do.

Ding. Ding. Ding.

Both Charles and Emma's cell phones illuminated as a group text filled their screens in rapid-fire.

Patty: J.D. should be at the clinic in a couple of minutes. I'm taking the grands home but let me know what's wrong with ol' Roscoe!

Bell: Oh, please keep me posted, too. It hurts my heart thinking of Roscoe in pain.

Bell: And J.D., too! He loves that old Lab so much.

As usual, Patty had anticipated J.D.'s timing. As Charles and Emma read the texts, a glow from the headlights of J.D.'s car shined into the lobby windows. It cast a spotlight on Poppy, who wagged her tail and stared out the clinic door.

Jingle. Jingle.

J.D. burst through the lobby door and rushed Roscoe to the exam room in the back. Poppy's head tilted when she saw the dog in J.D.'s arms, or maybe she could smell the clotted blood that had formed around the black Lab's wound. An animal's senses tell her what's happened long before humans get the message.

"You're going to be okay, old boy," J.D. promised.

In an instant, Charles went into triage mode while the bright, metal-rimmed medical light beamed down on the dog, who sat uneasily on the exam table. Charles' body moved fast and with focus, as his muscular physique bulged through his white vet's coat. With one hand, he prepared gauze and bandages, while the other hand checked the dog's legs and spine for any breaks.

Arley quietly stepped into the exam room. She and Emma had never met in person until this moment. They both stared in unison at the emergency response with eyes-wide-open, like they were watching an episode of *Grey's Anatomy*. They mostly used this room at the clinic for vaccinations and grooming—not as a doggy ER. J.D. remained calm, as always, and whispered soothing words to Roscoe. Their eyes connected. He massaged the dog's temples and rubbed his index finger around Roscoe's cheeks the way the dog liked. The room swirled with activity as Charles performed multiple medical tests while J.D. stood as strong as an oak tree withstanding a tornado.

Under the bright exam light, J.D. noticed gray fur around Roscoe's mouth. This was new—it certainly wasn't there when J.D. discovered the dog a few years back. The first time he'd ever seen Roscoe, the Labrador Retriever was riding in the back of a golf cart on the grounds of the community center. He perched on the cushy pad behind the driver's seat, where the security guards usually kept supplies. On that day, the only cargo was standing up on all four legs, tongue hanging out as he smiled in the breeze. J.D. wondered how he'd gotten back there and where he'd come from. No one seemed to know, not even the driver, who said *"He just jumped on board!"* Everyone wanted him around. The dog's past may have been unclear, but his future was solidified at that moment: Roscoe was welcome anytime and anywhere at the community center.

After that day, J.D. began noticing the dog all over campus. Early mornings, Roscoe followed the maintenance crew from building to building when they unlocked the doors to the center. It became a very fruitful ritual for the Lab. Vann and the rest of his team gave Roscoe bites of their egg sandwiches in the morning, then he'd usually gobble some ham from a cafeteria worker at lunchtime. On Tuesdays, the center offered free courses, and Mrs. Reeves always offered Roscoe a treat between teaching English classes. And J.D. gave the best head rubs. Each time he saw Roscoe, he'd rub his head and invite him inside his office, where the Lab stayed by his side. Roscoe chose his person. J.D. may have loved a lot of dogs in his life before this one, but he'd never connected like this.

Clunk. Clang. Zip.

Charles paused his exam, placing his equipment to the side, as though the half dozen tests he'd performed on the dog may have discovered something.

"What do you see, Charles? Is it a bite?" J.D. asked.

"J.D., I think it's a gunshot."

Emma gasped and clenched her chest. Arley awkwardly looked down at her own feet.

"Gunshot! What?" J.D. had navigated many crises in his career, always level-headed, but when he heard the word *gunshot* his blood ran cold.

"Thankfully, it didn't hit a vein or any organs. I know that much. But I need to x-ray him to figure out if it's a .22 bullet or a bb. There's no exit wound, so treatment depends on what's in there. As you can likely guess, one requires antibiotics. The other—" Charles paused. "Well, let's just hope it's a bb."

Arley stood in the corner of the exam room, shoulders slouched and head down, her hands cupping opposite elbows. In the doorway, Emma stood in her power pose, hands on her hips and head up as she assessed the room. To her, the nineteen-year-old hunched over in the corner was bad juju.

"Let's go brew some coffee while Charles and J.D. take care of Roscoe. These things can take time."

Dink. Dink.

Emma tapped the door frame with her ring, a silver band that encircled a red agate stone on her right ring finger. The sound startled Roscoe almost as much as Arley, who looked down at the floor of the exam room.

"Um, I'm good here," Arley said.

"It wasn't a question, baby girl. These folks need to care for that special dog. Let's go make some coffee."

As Emma watched Arley shrink into herself, it reminded her of the scared animals she sometimes saw at the clinic. They'd crouch low to the ground, trying to find safety when there was no nook to burrow in or no perch to climb. Emma forced a smile, calling on her charm to wrangle the anxiety-filled young woman. She knew Poppy's local celebrity could lure Arley out of the exam room.

"Poppy's treats are in the kitchen," she said. "I'll tell you all about how we rescued her if you come with me. I'll spill the good stuff, too. All the behind-the-scenes shenanigans you didn't read about in the group chats."

Arley pushed her hair behind her ear, rubbing her studded aqua earrings as she followed Emma into the kitchen. Poppy trailed them. She always trailed Emma, but especially when Emma walked toward the kitchen. Once inside, Emma moved like a symphony conductor as she filled a pot with water, scooped out some grounds, and hit start on the coffeemaker, all while pulling a dog treat out of a big blue drawer.

"This kitchen is filthy!" Emma said. She wiped down the countertop with a damp cloth, leaving behind an even shinier surface.

"Um, no. It's not filthy at all. I think everything looks so cute in here," Arley said, twirling one of the blue and white cabinet knobs.

"It may look clean, but you should see behind that refrigerator!"

Even if she could see behind the appliances, Arley would hardly notice. Her attention was focused on the three missed calls and eight texts from her mom that had come in since she left the community center. In the messages she learned her parents arrived at home, disappointed, and upset *"their only daughter"* wasn't waiting for them. "*You missed dinner,*" she wrote. "*It should be family first,*" she scolded. "*You have no respect for all we've done for you,*" led to "*I'm going to turn in early.*" Arley felt herself choking on guilt, but anger bubbled up too. Her mother completely forgot about her, and now she blamed Arley for being late to a dinner they never planned. "*Maybe they'll be less upset in the morning,*" she hoped. Her heart said she was where she needed to be, especially as she watched Emma dance around the kitchenette. As if on cue, Emma gracefully tossed a bag of treats to Arley. They both looked surprised that Arley caught it.

"Sit down and feed those to Poppy," Emma commanded.

"Sit? There are no chairs."

"Forget what I said about the dirt behind my refrigerator. My floor is clean!" She grabbed Arley's hand with a gentle squeeze; her red agate ring pressed coldly against Arley's fingers. Emma's deep brown eyes locked into Arley's hazel stare as she emphasized what she said next—not with her accent, but with her assurance.

"Trust me."

When Emma pulled back, Arley realized her palms filled with more dog treats. Emma nodded at the rug in the corner, knowing exactly what would happen when Arley sat down. Suddenly, the nineteen-year-old became the center of Poppy's universe as the holder of the treats. The little dog gobbled each one, as Emma told the tale of Poppy, who once captivated an entire town when back she was a timid lost pup on the side of Langston Road.

"For one full year, so many people tried to rescue Poppy, but only Bell could get close enough to pet her. She's the one who really sealed the deal. Charles and I were just reinforcements," Emma said proudly.

"Does Charles ever worry that she'll wander off again? Try to go back to the woods?"

"Oh, no. She rules the roost here at the clinic. And she'd miss Charles' belly rubs. He spoils her."

Poppy's frame had grown much fuller than it was back when Emma sent regular updates and pictures of the stray to Charles and Bell via a group text. The friends were practically strangers then, and now most people assumed Charles and Emma were much more than business partners, even if she wouldn't "put a label on it," as she told anyone daring enough to ask her relationship status. Without the little dog, Emma, Charles, and Bell may never have met. Hanging over the coffeemaker was a photo of Charles in front of the flatbed truck he used to drive hauling timber. It served as a "memorial to all the trees he killed," Emma explained. For Charles, the photo reminded him daily during his cup of black coffee that life got so much better when he stopped living alone on the highway.

Giggle. Giggle. Ha!

"Stop it!" Arley chuckled, laughing uncontrollable on the floor.

"Emma! Help!"

With no more treats left in her hands, Poppy switched to puppy-kisses mode, licking Arley's hands and neck. She seemed fond of the studded-aqua earrings Arley wore.

"Oh, Poppy! Give that child a break!"

Arley's laugh emoted pure joy. She leapt up to her feet as she thanked Poppy for the love and wiped the slobber off her earrings.

"I like those stones, Arley. Looks like aquamarine?"

"How did you know?"

"I know a thing or two about gemstones. Those should bring—"

"Happiness," they said together.

"Ah, I think we may have something in common! Come check out my store. You can pick any stone you want on the house."

Poppy followed the women to the lobby, where Emma flipped a switch that illuminated all of the colorful polished gemstones she'd collected over the years. Some were woven into pet accessories for good luck, others were just piled in boxes with their purpose written in gold ink on the backdrop.

"This feels magical!" Arley exclaimed, rolling the stones in her hand to pick just the right one. "I can really pick any stone I want?"

"Baby girl, you can pick two."

She chose one from a box marked "Hope" and another from a box marked "Courage," the same stone Emma had called on when deciding to change her name.

"Good choices. I believe we're kindred spirits, Arley. Are you going to be in town for long?"

"For the summer."

"You can come back to my shop anytime," she said as a tail thumped between them. "Poppy loves visitors."

"Can I ask you something, Emma?"

"Sure. I'm a tightly guarded open book."

"What was in that box marked "Protection?"

"Oh, that's one of my favorites. Red agate. I used to leave it out on the side of the road back when we were all trying to lure Poppy in from the woods. I'd leave those stones all over Langston Road to help watch over her."

"Red agate?" Arley reached into her pocket and pulled out a red and black gemstone. "Does it look like this?"

"That's red agate! It's been very popular lately. One of the vet techs said someone came in today and bought the entire box. That's why the "Protection" bin is empty. I'll tumble a new batch this weekend."

Arley looked uneasy.

"When we discovered someone shot Roscoe," she said, "I found this piece by the spot where he bled the most."

"Look at that! Well...sounds like it did his job. That dog is going to be okay."

"There's more to it than that." Arley reached into the pockets of her baggy, black-linen jumpsuit, digging deep. "See?"

Both of Arley's hands overflowed with red agate stones. She emptied them all into the box marked "Protection" filling it back up to the brim.

"These were all where Roscoe was shot?" Emma asked.

"Every one of them. Do you think whoever shot Roscoe bought these stones here?"

Thud. Thud. Thud. Thud.

Roscoe's heavy steps interrupted Arley's investigation as he limped out of the exam room with Charles and J.D. trailing behind him.

"We have a diagnosis," J.D. said, looking relieved, "Antibiotics for ten days...and lots of extra treats for Roscoe."

"He's going to be fine," Charles said. "We're going to leave that bb inside him. It's a safer approach than surgery at his age. But we need to give him antibiotics while the wound heals up. What a tough Lab he is!"

"Now that we know what happened," J.D. declared, "We're moving on to who did this."

Emma stared at the empty box of gemstones, then over at the smiling Lab, then back up at J.D. She gripped her elbows, stepping backwards from the group. For Emma, the past came back in a hail of red agate. She leaned against the wall, knowing all too well who pulled the trigger, but she felt too triggered herself to say a word.

CHAPTER 4

The Presentation

Click. Tap. Snap.

J.D. and Patty's preparation routine moved with a staccato rhythm of checks, balances, and reminders. They sorted through stacks of papers, binders, and note cards scattered across the office that led up to the day's big event. They packed and unpacked the necessities J.D. would need for his presentation at the podium.

"Your speech?" Patty asked.

"Got it," J.D. confirmed.

"Phone charger?"

"Right here."

"Breath check?"

J.D. raised his eyebrow and asked, "Do I need a mint?"

"I meant for Roscoe," Patty said. "I'm not sure Commissioner Bankston is going to appreciate a dog at the table."

North Star Community Center buzzed with anticipation ahead of the state commissioner's arrival, and J.D. carried the responsibility on his shoulders that his boss' visit would not only go well, but go flawlessly. Every summer, Commissioner Bankston named his choice for the top performing community center in the entire state. Part of the honor for the winner included hosting the annual planning meeting. After the celebration of being selected came weeks of hard work getting ready for visitors. They transformed the lobby of the theater into an event space worthy of a summer gala. Every detail dripped with elegance. Large balloons floated up toward the ceiling like giant champagne bubbles, and ribbons lined the staircase banister. Lace and sparkle adorned every detail, and the meeting space was as colorful as a Christmas present. The room dazzled, and J.D. wanted the extraordinary setting to impress his boss. He'd planned to use the occasion to request funding from the commissioner for a bronze statue of North Star's mascot, a valiant mustang frozen mid-gallop. He envisioned it would stand larger-than-life in the center of campus, adding culture to the facility while making a statement that North Star was a workhorse for the community. Seeing Roscoe sprawled out across the floor of the administration building reminded J.D. that his current focus should be on another animal. One that Patty feared had breath so foul it may offend his boss.

"I don't know that it's a real good idea to have a dog in my office when the commissioner arrives," J.D. said, looking down at Roscoe.

Ever since the shooting two weeks ago, Roscoe hadn't left J.D.'s side. Or maybe J.D. hadn't left his. The pair became inseparable. Roscoe spent his time in J.D.'s office on the corduroy dog bed that Bell had picked out for him. She chose the material thinking that it would feel good on his wounded leg, which seemed to heal just fine despite having a bb permanently lodged inside it. In fact, Roscoe seemed mostly unaffected by his injury, although the attack had put J.D. on high alert. He scanned security camera footage from around the community center and confirmed that whoever fired the shot had pulled the trigger off campus. However, in one video he found something concerning. A man in red flannel followed Roscoe as the dog limped through campus. The video showed this man throwing rocks at the dog. No one recognized the man from the footage, but the security team stayed on alert in case he returned, and they posted his blurry photo all over campus.

"Maybe the commissioner likes dogs," Patty said.

"He probably loves dogs."

"That breath though," Patty waved her hand over her nose.

During the commissioner's visit, they set Roscoe up in an empty office down the hall. This insured the old black Lab remained safe and also kept him out of view during the big meeting. Mayors, heads of industry, and every community center director in the region attended. This meeting was no place for a dog, especially since J.D. planned to ask his boss to fund the mustang statue.

Within an hour, the campus filled with dignitaries and leaders from across the state. They gathered beneath the bubbling balloons, sipping on punch from a crystal bowl nestled just beneath an ice sculpture of a galloping mustang—a small but significant detail designed to help sell the commissioner on the statue. While the room swirled with people, J.D. slipped away from the crowd and into the office at the end of the hall.

"Doing ok, old boy?"

Roscoe looked up at him and smiled, his tail thumping on the tile floor.

"I'll be back to let you out as soon as this is over. We'll take a ride in the golf cart together."

Roscoe's tail thumped louder, and J.D. turned away and closed the door behind him. After confirmation that his special friend was content, J.D. felt ready to deliver the annual report to the crowd, heralding the triumphs of the past year. From the podium, he touted record enrollment in outreach programs. They'd provided the fastest free Wi-Fi in ten counties and reading programs to help anyone who needed it. He declared the new softball stadium a gift to the region, offering a state-of-the-art sports complex for schools lacking their own. And he announced the return of the Latino Festival, coming back to North Star Community Center in just two weeks. What started a decade ago as a food truck selling tamales next to a mariachi band grew into the largest cultural celebration of its kind in the state. Sensing he impressed the crowd with the list of accomplishments, J.D.'s heart raced as he took advantage of the momentum. He decided to ask the commissioner to fund the statue in front of the entire crowd. How could he say no?

"And finally," said J.D., as he began his pitch, "I'd like to speak about the future."

A hush covered the room as they waited to hear J.D.'s next idea for North Star.

"Envision a place in the center of campus, decorated with a work of art worthy of placement in an Atlanta sculpture hall."

Click!

As he neared the peak of his pitch, the door to the event hall latched open, echoing through the silent room.

"We can build this work of art together. It will be a sculpture where the community comes first. This will be a conversation piece commissioned with your support."

J.D. looked around the room to connect with the full audience. If he hadn't been so focused on nailing his pitch, he might have looked back to see who had walked through the door to the reception.

"This will be more than a statue; it will tell your story...and yours...and yours. The statue will tell *our* story as one community."

J.D. noticed he was losing the attention of some attendees sitting at the tables in the back. In the far corner, he saw a whir of movement as his team raced around, bent over, and rushing as though they were trying to catch a bug.

Boom! Thud!

Suddenly, the sounds of the hall door slamming diverted everyone's attention from the podium. It closed so hard a sonic boom seemed to echo through the space. The guests stopped eating and drinking, craning their necks to see what happened, and the loud clinking of forks and glasses added to the growing chaos. Steady footsteps scraped on the tile floor, yet no one could see this mysterious visitor.

Tap. Tap. Tap. Tap.

Head-turns and sideways glances rolled across the crowd, cascading like people doing the wave in a football stadium. Finally, even those on the opposite side of the room saw the unexpected visitor. With a smile on their faces, the dignitaries' focus shifted from J.D. to an old, black Lab. Somehow, Roscoe had escaped from his temporary holding area in the empty office and found his person giving a presentation to a room full of strangers. It didn't faze the dog much. Roscoe walked through the crowd as though it was a common occurrence. A good dog doesn't recognize politicians, leaders of commerce, or even a state commissioner; he just knows his person. And this good dog headed straight for J.D., who quickly pivoted to improvise the rest of his speech with a guest dog at the luncheon.

"Folks, meet Roscoe! Our unofficial ambassador!"

The crowd was unsure if J.D. had planned this canine cameo. A few people clapped. Others took photos with their phones. From across the room Patty locked eyes with J.D. and, as if she could read his mind, she mouthed, *"I'm so sorry! I tried to catch him!"* In fact, Chad, Brenda, Trish, and most of the team had raced around the hallways of the community center, desperate to prevent Roscoe and his bad breath from busting into the gala. Even at his old age, Roscoe knew how to evade them all.

J.D. watched the crowd and assessed how to handle the unexpected disruption. He thought to himself, *"If I tried to stop him now, I'd look foolish chasing a dog around."* So, as always, J.D. let Roscoe be Roscoe. As he continued with his presentation, Roscoe walked over to the commissioner and plopped down on the floor next to him. It was as though he knew the man was J.D.'s boss. Roscoe was accustomed to sitting in the VIP section, and that's what he did for the rest of the presentation. His tail flapped right on top of Commissioner Bankston's polished loafers. After J.D.'s speech, the Lab walked back through the crowd and left the building; nothing could entertain him after hearing his person speak.

Roscoe's appearance seemed to have lightened the air. One by one, the two-hundred-forty-eight guests in the audience returned to their fancy cars, sure to tell the story of the sweet old dog who stole the show. However jovial the crowd seemed; they hadn't heard J.D.'s official request for funding. He told everyone about the vision for the statue, but when the dog took over the show, he decided it wasn't the best time to ask his boss about spending money. On Commissioner Bankston's way out, he stopped at the podium, shook J.D.'s hand and said just five words: *"Great job. I love dogs."* Then, the commissioner was whisked away in a black SUV, followed soon by a line of other dignitaries, who departed from the community center as quickly as they descended.

Hours passed, and the decorations came down. Only J.D. and Roscoe remained in the reception hall, with its lights dimmed in after-hours mode. Outside, the grand fountain flickered with reflecting pops of purple and green light.

"At least we have a nice fountain," J.D. muttered to himself, certain his dream of building the mustang statue ended.

Whoosh. Whoosh. Whoosh.

He brushed an industrial broom across the floor as Roscoe followed behind him, occasionally chasing the bristles. It was a dance between friends who worked and played together.

"J.D. Campbell, what are you doing sweeping floors?" Patty exclaimed, switching on the bright lights to the reception hall. "And in the dark!"

"There was no work left to do, so I thought I could help clean up."

"You have people for that. When there is no work to do, you go home!"

"I'll just be a little longer," he said, playfully leading Roscoe left to right with the broom. "I want to do my part. Besides, I enjoy spending time with Roscoe."

Ever since the shooting, J.D. let Roscoe spend the night on the dog bed he kept across from his desk. Bell set up a little camera that allowed them to check in on him from time to time. Darrell, the groundskeeper, installed a doggy door in case Roscoe needed some fresh air during the night. So far, Roscoe was content, and that offered peace of mind to J.D. His dog would have a safe place to go if he tired of roaming across the mountain. After just one night in the cozy office, Roscoe seemed to have declared it home.

"Look at your phone, J.D." Patty said. "Your speech is blowing up!"

His eyes widened as he asked, "What do you mean?"

"Just check your phone."

J.D. reached in his pocket, realizing he'd silenced his phone so it wouldn't ring during his presentation. As he powered it on, messages blasted on screen. Everyone was texting about his presentation and, specifically, how Roscoe made himself a part of it.

Ding. Ding. Ding.

Charles: Everyone's talking about Roscoe here at the animal clinic. You've got to see this picture going around!

Bell: Is he ok?

Charles: Ok? He's internet-famous! They're calling him a star! Emma, do you have a link?

There was no reply from her, which is quite unusual for the most active texter in the group.

Buzz. Buzz. Blip.

J.D.'s social media alerts fired off, too. He'd been tagged in a post, already shared hundreds of times. It showed J.D. at the podium smiling down at Roscoe, who was curled up at the feet of the commissioner. Someone had captioned it *"The star of North Star."*

"Well, how about that!"

"Roscoe's gone viral!" Patty said. "But did you read the comments? That's the good stuff."

As J.D. read the comments, he saw people sharing personal stories about Roscoe. The canine seemed to be an unofficial therapy dog for many. A young mother confessed how nervous she felt when she first moved to the area, but she leaned on the community center for the support she needed to find job training. She wrote, *"When I saw Roscoe on campus, I thought if they have a dog, it can't be that scary there."* Now, she works from home for a data research center. Others shared stories about how the first thing their children want to do when they go to sporting events at the community center is *"pet the old, black Lab hanging around the ball field."* Another tagged a group of friends who met each other after they realized they all had been saving scraps from their lunch as take out for the dog. *"Now we eat together every day, and Roscoe probably gets one bite for every bite we take."*

"Dogs are about the greatest ice breaker there is," J.D. said as he looked away from his phone and over at Roscoe. "You made quite the impression today, old boy!"

Roscoe sat on his hind legs, wagged his tail, and give a slobbery smile.

"We're never locking him in an empty office again. He'll have free rein on campus," J.D. declared. "After all, he's our most popular ambassador."

"Smartest one, too—" said Patty. "He gets you to do whatever he wants. That dog trained *you.*"

Ding. Ding.

Charles: I found the link! Click here.

Bell: This is just wonderful!

In the group text, Bell and Charles had shared the link to a local news article, which had already published a report online. The headline read,

"*Community Center Director Announces Dog Statue at North Star.*"

"Have you seen this one, Patty? A dog statue! I think they must have combined my speech about the mustang statue with Roscoe's surprise appearance."

"Are you thinking what I'm thinking?"

"We need to come up with the money for that statue. It may not be exactly what I had in mind, but—" J.D. paused as he felt Roscoe sinking down on the floor by his feet. "This is going to be even better."

Buzz. Whoosh.

One last message came around the group text thread: *Emma has left the chat.*

Emma had created that text thread years ago, when the group of friends set out to rescue Poppy from Langston Road. Now, the friends texted each other there almost every day with dog pics or updates about Poppy or the clinic. It made little sense that she'd leave the chat.

Ding.

Charles: Something is wrong with Emma. I've lost her. Bell, please come over.

CHAPTER 5

It's Over

"Please don't ruin this for me, Charles. Please don't make it harder than it already is."

In a frenzy, Emma snapped open the lid to a large plastic storage bin. She estimated she'd need three more to pack up all her gemstones from her corner booth at the clinic.

They were the only two people left at the clinic after Emma had closed the entire practice down early and sent the staff home. She blamed the change on technical difficulties with the accounting software. As soon as the vet techs drove away from the parking lot, it became clear to Charles that the only glitch was of the human variety. Something was wrong with Emma. Something big.

"Please, just tell me what's wrong," Charles said, but his plea was interrupted by a sudden escape.

Dogs of all sizes escaped from their pens and circled the inside of the clinic in a parade of excitement. One of the vet techs had accidentally left the main latch on the kennel door unlocked. Charles chased after a beagle, then a doodle, then a redbone hound. He was getting nowhere, unable to reel in any of them. And that's when Emma, standing in the center of a circle of galloping canines, gave her business partner notice. Emma told Charles she'd be handing over her share of the clinic to him, effective immediately.

"All of it," she said.

"You want to put me in the past, but I won't let you do that," he gasped. "It doesn't make sense, Emma. We own this business together. You can't just walk away."

"I'd agree with you, Charles. But then we'd both be wrong. It's over. Keep the clinic. It's yours now. I'm packing up and moving on. Maybe I'll go to Florida. I hear Gulfport's nice."

She placed the plastic bin on a vintage bar stool Emma salvaged from the old soda stand at H&H Pharmacy. She must have tumbled a thousand gemstones while sitting on that stool, and she loved it. Emma would sip on her Coca-Cola and snack on a "Hurr-sheey bar," her Southern accent somehow made the chocolate sound so much more divine. But today the stool was being used as a loading dock. The vinyl seat cover creaked as Emma swirled the stool around by its chrome base and loaded up another bin of merchandise.

Clunk. Clunk. Rumble.

She threw handfuls of crystals into the container with no order or care, then poured a box of bright blue rocks down on top of them. Charles struggled to slip a leash over the escaped doodle while he lifted a runaway beagle up under his arm.

"Why are you doing this?"

"I've gone through every scenario, Charles. I promise the ending always stays the same. If I leave now, maybe you have a chance—"

Bark! Bark! Crash!

The doodle broke free of the leash, bounded over the front counter barrier, and began devouring a bowl of treats next to the register. Meanwhile, the redbone hound pushed open the kennel door, freeing three more dogs to run wild through the clinic.

"It feels like there's something you're not telling me, Emma. You can tell me anything."

"Let me spell it out for you, Charles. I can't be your friend. I can't be your partner. I can't be the reason you don't live a happy life."

"I don't understand. Have I upset you? I thought I had a happy life."

Emma didn't answer. Or even look up. She was consumed by a determination to extract her shop from their clinic. In a matter of minutes, she filled three more plastic bins with merchandise, leaving the entire booth empty. The rocks, meticulously sorted when on display, were now haphazardly mixed together in the bins, like a box of names shuffled for a giveaway drawing. Usually, she handled each stone individually and with a black felt cloth, out of respect for the rock's essence and intention. But now the stones clinked together like a jumble of glass bottles meant for recycling.

As she attempted to move the stack of bins through the lobby, a line of dogs darted past her. She tripped and knocked the top box onto the hard tile. Blue, green, and crystal-colored gemstones spilled across the clinic floor like a bag of rice opened upside down. The spill sent Emma to her knees, grasping at stones.

"Emma! Are you ok?"

Charles rushed to her side, reaching his arm around her shoulder as her body caved into his. One by one, tears streamed down her face faster than she could wipe them away. Words didn't flow, just the emotion. As Charles held her, a dozen dogs bounced around the clinic. They gobbled up treats, shredded paper towels, and ripped puppy pads in a playful tug-of-war. Dog toys, office supplies, and grooming materials were collateral damage. Charles ignored the canine takeover and kept his attention on Emma. She could only hear the self-critical thoughts in her mind and curled into the fetal position on the clinic floor. Pets left in their care swirled around them in a hurricane of interspecies excitement mixed with human despair.

Jingle. Jingle.

The bells over the front door shook as someone entered the clinic. On the floor, Charles' vantage point was blocked. The dogs didn't notice that a new human had entered the lobby—except for Poppy, who ran to the center of the room wagging her tail and spinning in joy.

"Hello?" Charles called out, his voice muffled by the sound of yapping dogs.

The visitor replied with a hush, emitting a soft sound just above a whisper that slowly coated the room.

"Shhhhhhhhhhhhhhhh..."

The dogs ignored the soothing sound, but the visitor kept going.

"Shhhhhhhhhhhhhhhh..."

The beagle stopped shredding the roll of paper towels in the corner.

"Shhhhhhhhhhhhhhhh..."

The doodle stopped searching for more treats. Then Poppy belted out a howl as loud as the voice was soft.

"Oooo-oooo-ooooooooooo!" Poppy exclaimed.

Charles saw a hand hold two fingers up in the air. His eyes followed the hand as it walked back to the kennel with every dog in the clinic following behind in formation.

"Shhhhhhhhhhhhhhh..."

The sound continued, even from the other room. Other noises joined in along the way, like a percussion section playing out of rhythm.

Thud! Clink. Click. Thud! Clink. Click.

Charles heard latches closing, cage by cage, until one final click ended the chaos. All the dogs were safely back in the kennel, except for Poppy. She was standing about three feet away from Emma and Charles by the great dog wrangler's side. Charles looked up, finally close enough to see that the mysterious puppy whisperer was their dear friend.

"Bell!" he said, careful not to disturb Emma.

But the sound of her friend's name caught Emma's attention.

"Bell?"

Emma slowly lifted her head as Poppy licked the salty tears from her skin. She felt the dog's heart racing even faster than her own as Emma scratched the pup. The thumping rhythm of Poppy's wagging tail helped ease the tension in Emma's chest. The crushing burden she'd carried inside remained but, for the moment, she could breathe again. Wagging the worries away is a magic trick dogs perform on humans all the time.

"I need to tell both of you something," said Emma. "But I'm not ready."

"Is it okay if I sit with you until you are?" Bell asked, kneeling next to her. Her petite frame folded down to the ground gracefully. Emma rested her head on Bell's shoulder as Charles supported her back. Poppy folded in with the three friends. The dog curled in front of Emma on the cold, clinic floor. Towering around them, plastic bins haphazardly filled with Emma's gemstone inventory cast a shadow across the lobby. The clinic was now quiet, and the trio sat together in silence for a minute, then two...but no more than five minutes passed before Emma began to fidget.

"This floor isn't very comfortable," she said.

"We're staying here with you," Charles insisted. "If you're uncomfortable, we'll be uncomfortable with you."

"It's just...I mean, when's the last time you mopped, Charles? This is a vet clinic. We must be sitting on a lot of—" she whispered the next part, "animal feces residue."

Poppy appeared to give her a puppy side eye.

"I scrub this floor every day, Emma!"

"I can get you a clean blanket," Bell offered. "You know, for something soft to sit on."

"No, no. We can sit here just fine," Emma said, as she shifted her body again. "This just seems sort of silly though, doesn't it? The three of us curled up on the floor?"

"Tell me you're kidding?" Charles said.

"It's funny. But I'm not joking. We shouldn't be down on this filthy floor!"

"Don't judge your own come apart, Emma. Do what you need," Bell said. "We'll sit with you as long as you want."

Emma's mind processed her options, and she decided it was time to put a wrap on her breakdown and share her truth. She slowly stood, pulling Charles and Bell with her. Next, she smoothed the wrinkles from her denim skirt and brushed a few strands of dog fur off her black V-neck to look presentable. With her hands firmly planted on her hips, elbows bent and shoulders back, the time felt right to confess the secret she'd packed away in all those plastic bins.

"It's my fault Roscoe was shot."

A confused expression washed over their faces as Charles and Bell looked at each other, concerned for Emma as she declared "I realize we can't be friends anymore, Bell. I know how J.D. feels about that dog. This is unforgivable."

"How could *you* have been involved in that? You were here with Charles when it happened," asked Bell.

"Emma, that confession makes about as much sense as Mother Nature gave a rock. We all saw the security camera of footage of the man who did it. You're not even five and a half feet tall in shoes. Unless you walked on paint cans and stuffed a red flannel shirt with about a hundred pounds of potatoes, I don't think there's an Emma connection."

"*I* didn't shoot him—"

Her voice commanded the room, echoing through the lobby. Even Poppy locked her eyes on Emma as they all waited for her to finish her thought.

"But I know who did." Her head tilted down to the floor. She couldn't even make eye contact with Poppy, much less Bell and Charles. "I think maybe he did it to send me a message. I can prove it."

Emma marched over to the plastic container in the far corner, popped back the blue lid and pulled out a cardboard box with the word "Protection" on it.

"See?" she said, shaking the empty box as she held it out closer to Bell and Charles.

She explained how someone purchased all of her red agate in one day. The vet tech made the sale while Emma did payroll. The mystery shopper bought every red stone in the collection. Back then, Emma wrote it off as a good day. She thought nothing more of it until Arley pulled a fistful of the red gemstones from her pocket that she found near a puddle of blood where Roscoe had been injured.

"Emma, I diagnosed Roscoe," Charles explained, "He was shot with a bb. Rocks didn't cause him to bleed. It's just a coincidence that someone bought all your red agate."

"Where else is somebody going to get that around here, Charles? This isn't Fraggle Rock! I'm the only person who sells this woo-woo stuff in Jackson County."

"Even if that man bought the rocks from you," reasoned Bell, "You're not to blame. You can't control what people do once they buy something from you."

"It's not *what* he did with the gemstones. It's *who* he is," she said. "I—I don't even want to say his name."

Emma squatted down and wrapped her arm around Poppy for comfort once again.

"You don't have to," Bell said.

"I don't want to say his name—but I will. You're my people."

"We'll get through it together," Charles assured her. "You can say anything to me."

"The man's first name, if my theory is correct, is Xavier. It's been seventeen years since I last spoke with him. Seventeen years since he filled my gas tank with the red agate gemstones I planned to sell at the Art Sunday Festival. And seventeen years since he disappeared in the middle of the night."

"Oh, Emma," Charles' eyes widened.

"And seventeen years later my last name is still the same as his."

Emma slowly stood up and stared out the lobby window, her back to Bell and Charles. Poppy followed, and leaned against her leg, her face looking toward them.

"Charles, do you know Xavier?" Bell whispered. "I'm confused."

"I—I—" Charles tried to speak softly, but his deep voice carried through the room. He didn't want Emma to hear them speaking about her past.

"Uh-hmmm."

The sound of Emma clearing her throat cut him off. She was still looking outside the window, taking a moment to process. Clearly, she wasn't ready for commentary. Charles typed a message into his cell phone. Without making a sound, he mouthed, *"Check your texts."*

Ding. Ding. Ding. Ding.

The room stayed silent, other than the beeps and buzzing of Charles and Bell's text conversation.

Ding. Ding.

Bell gasped when she read his explanation of who this man is. Charles shushed her, as politely as he could.

Ding.

"Sorry!" he texted.

After more silence, Emma quickly spun back around, as though she'd come up for air from whatever alternative plane of consciousness she'd been hiding within.

"I know you two are texting about me," she quipped. "You can stop. I'm ready to tell you everything. The fact of the matter is Xavier is a man that I thought was gone for good. For seventeen years I believed that, even in the early days when I prayed he'd come back. Now that he really has, I think what he did to Roscoe has something to do with me. That's because the connection between Xavier and me is..."

Even Poppy seemed to wait for her confession.

"He's Sia's father."

Emma's eyes didn't look away this time as the tears ran down her face. She stood stoically with her shoulders back and face up high, ready to accept her punishment after she expressed her biggest fear to the world, even if only her two closest friends could hear.

"Oh, Emma," Bell touched her arm, her blue eyes filled with empathy. Emma stood stiff, staring at Charles. He looked around the room like an animal trapped in a cage, as though his mind couldn't latch on to what to do next, until an idea hit.

"You need sangria!"

In a frenzy, he led his two friends out through the kennel, parading Poppy passed the yapping dogs until the trio exited the clinic through the back door. They walked across the puppy play area and made their way to his cabin next door. From there, he swirled up the fastest pitcher of red sangria he'd ever made. Sitting on the porch, each with a glass in hand, Charles and Bell listened to Emma tell the story of how things had fallen apart with her ex.

"We were business partners in the beginning, filled with dreams of dollar signs and trips around the globe," she explained.

It all changed when Sia was born. That's when Emma decided that instead of working for travel money, she wanted their jewelry company to focus on ways to make the world a better place for their child. They became a family divided by direction. Xavier wanted to cut costs to raise profits so the family would be more secure, even if it meant misleading customers.

"I remember once he suggested I paint pieces of broken concrete and tell people it was gemstones. He'd do anything to make a buck from a penny," Emma recalled.

The disagreement over their company's mission grew into a great philosophical divide about something far more important. Money was just part of what they fought about. When Sia was an infant, Xavier became more detached—he wouldn't even hold his own child. *"That's a mama's job,"* he'd say. Months passed, the profits kept dipping lower, and neglect turned into mental abuse. He'd say little things to discourage Emma, etching away at her confidence as a mother and as an entrepreneur. She thought maybe he was right; maybe she was worthless in either role.

With their savings almost completely drained on rent, diapers, and just enough gemstones for one last go at her dream, Emma bet it all. She had faith she could launch a shop selling her artisan crystal kits. No one was doing anything like it in the entire county—not even at Jim Pitts' Gifts, which was known as the place for everything special back then. Her plan was to sell them at stores all over the region from Mississippi to Atlanta. Emma designed a kit for inner peace, another for prosperity, and her favorite—the red agate kit for protection. She spent an entire month tumbling unpolished rocks into gemstones. By the time she sent a pitch deck to a few stores in Birmingham, she had hundreds of kits ready to ship. It would be enough money to start a fund for Sia's education.

"He had me convinced we were a family all in on it together, from the baby to the business. I'd mail out samples to all the stores, but Xavier assigned himself to be the closer," Emma explained.

"Closer? Like, he'd close the store at night?" Bell asked.

"No, closer as in the one to close the deal. He'd call up every store to ask how many orders they wanted to place," Emma paused. "I wanted to call them myself. I see myself as a closer. But he wanted to be the big man making it happen."

"I can't imagine you not doing anything you want to do," said Charles.

"Well, I told myself it made more sense for him to do it. As if being a man made him more influential," she scoffed. "But it seemed to make him happy. And it gave me more time to take care of the baby. He had no interest in doing any of that."

Emma sent out kit after kit, and Xavier began to travel—from Mississippi to Atlanta. He told her he visited store after store in person to close the deal, and every single shop gave the same answer. "*Not a match.*" They all passed on the opportunity to sell her gemstone kits.

"He delighted in telling me that one store owner laughed at the idea. I felt like a fool. Then an email changed everything."

Bell leaned in, hanging on her every word. She rubbed the back of Poppy's neck, who seemed smitten her three people were all on the porch with her.

"What was in the email, Emma?" Bell asked.

"One store emailed me directly. I guess they tracked me down through our website, because the pitch I sent had his email on it. Remember, he was the alleged closer."

She explained that the store owner ordered fifty crystal sets. Then another place reached out and ordered thirty-five. Then came another and another. Emma didn't reveal any of this to Xavier right away. Instead, she began investigating. She discovered those stores couldn't have turned down her proposals, because he never actually visited a single location.

"To this day, I don't know where he really went when he said he was traveling to Atlanta."

"So, he'd been lying all along?" Bell asked. "Why?"

"Now that is the question for the ages, isn't it?" Emma said. "I think maybe for control. He wanted me to believe his ideas worked and mine were worthless."

"This is what you taught me about, isn't it, Emma? Gaslighting?" Charles asked. "When someone manipulates your reality by telling you that you are the one with the issue."

"Yep," she held up her near-empty glass and swirled the last sip of sangria. "I thought my business burnt out. Turns out, he was turning the lights off on me."

She explained how he got violent after she confronted him with the truth. He ripped her pitch decks into shreds and busted apart her workshop. He never laid a hand on her or their child, but everything in his body showed that he could. Just like his father used to abuse him. Emma knew it was over. She told him the outbursts had to stop, or else she'd leave...and he vanished.

"But not without a parting gift," Emma tossed back the final swig of sangria. "It almost destroyed my old Saturn. I loved that car almost as much as my Jeep!"

She still remembers the look on the mechanic's face when her car broke down half-way to Huntsville. He told Emma that inside her gas tank, instead of 88 octane, she had a pile of red agate gemstones blocking her fuel line. He'd taken them from the crystal kits she had ready to ship.

"Xavier plopped them in, one by one. After the mechanic fished them out, they smelled flammable. I couldn't fulfill my orders without those rocks. I had to refund every store. By the time I spent the next month's rent money to restock most of the stores lost interest," she said. Emma's usually animated face looked blank, as though the memory chained her to a place she didn't want to be. "He tried to wreck my car, but what happened was I got wrecked."

"Why did he do that?" Bell asked. "How could he do that to you?"

"Sounds like he's mean-hearted," Charles grumbled, barely over a whisper.

"He knew it would hurt me. And I suppose, like all of us, something had hurt him deep down to his core. The world makes us how we are," Emma said.

"Correction. Sounds like he's a mean-hearted fool," Charles said. He spoke louder this time, almost in a bark. It made Poppy jump.

"I didn't see "mean-hearted fool" on my bingo card, yet that's what I got. But I got Sia, too. I wouldn't change a thing. He wasn't that way in the beginning. Or maybe he was, and I was too blinded his attention to know. Thinking about how I missed that side of him keeps me up at night."

"What does Sia think of him?" Bell asked.

"Sia doesn't even know him. She was too young when he left, and he never once tried to get in touch. Oh, God, is he going to try to meet her?"

Suddenly, from the dark countryside stretched out around the porch, bright headlights shone in the driveway. It startled them, but Poppy seemed unbothered.

Thump. Thump. Thump.

Their eyes couldn't see past the light as the driver slid out of the vehicle, kicking gravel up as he scurried toward them.

Thump. Thump. Thump. Thump.

With each footstep, Poppy's brown tail wagged faster, echoing on the wooden porch as her body wiggled in glee. Faster than a hiccup, she ran over to the familiar face who had just arrived.

"J.D., I can explain—" Emma said, misunderstanding why he arrived. She reacted like the sheriff had shown up at a speakeasy.

Instead of scolding her, J.D. rested his arm on Emma's shoulder. She exhaled a mountain of worry.

"Emma, Bell texted me about your news tonight. She must have sent me twenty messages. I came here so you'd know you have nothing to explain. We're good."

"I'm just so sorry, J.D. And Roscoe! You know I'd never do anything to hurt him, don't you? He's like family!"

"You're like family. And there's something I want to make sure you hear, Emma." J.D. looked directly in Emma's eyes as his voice lowered. "The only connection you have to Roscoe's attack is that you know how it feels to be bullied by this guy, too."

J.D. had a way about him that eased the most worried mind. Emma nodded and mouthed the words *"Thank you"* before turning to the group to make an announcement.

"I apologize for the theatrics, everyone. You could say my actions tonight were PTSD rearing its ugly head. I'm mortified, but...I'm not going anywhere."

"There's no reason to be embarrassed about anything around us," Charles said as he draped his arm on Emma's shoulder. He felt warm, and she felt safe again with her people beside her.

"Rage and hope can live side by side," she said, pulling a piece of red agate out of her pocket. "And I can promise you this tonight: It's over. It. Is. Over. I'll keep Xavier from causing heartache around here a second time."

"Now Emma, you don't want to get in a spraying contest with a skunk," Charles said.

"Sure I do, Charles. I just have to cause a bigger stink!"

"But this guy is dangerous. He shot Roscoe. I'm afraid to think about what he might to do you."

"Don't worry, Charles. I can handle myself."

Bark!

Poppy seemed to agree.

"Now you all get out of here. The clinic will be open at eight in the morning, and I need to get my rock store looking presentable again! I need to clean this place up."

Charles smiled, "*We* need to clean it up, partner."

CHAPTER 6

A Banner Year

Time moves differently for a dog. Instead of clocks, canines capture moments with their senses. Dogs know when something's coming well before humans. The scent of a steak sizzling blocks away sends them roaming across a neighborhood to track down a taste. Their vision detects patterns in movement and assigns meaning. If their person reaches for a leash, they know a walk to the park is coming. Grabbing keys means their person is leaving. Sounds help a dog predict what's next, like the pop of a food can opening or, as on this summer morning, the click of a car door closing in the parking lot outside North Star Community Center.

Click. Click. Slam!

Roscoe looked up when he heard the ordinary sound that, to a human, could be any driver pulling up to the center on this special June day. Yet Roscoe distinguished the driver from sound alone, even from within J.D.'s corner office. The old Lab yawned as the morning light beamed through the blinds. He was not accustomed to such an early arrival, especially on a Saturday. He watched the doorway with a slobbery smile of anticipation, ears perked forward as they tracked the approaching footsteps.

Pat. Pat. Pat.

The distinct pace sent Roscoe to his feet and the Lab's thick, barrel-shaped body wiggled from his tail to his tongue as the latch of the door handle clicked: His person was here.

"Roscoe! Good morning, ol' boy!"

He wiggled so hard his front legs lifted off the ground, like he wanted to stand up and hug J.D. around the neck. A head rub would do, and J.D. scratched the spot between his ears that made Roscoe whimper in delight.

"I bet you wonder what I'm doing here so early, don't you, boy? Want to go for a ride to find out?"

Roscoe knew that word "ride" and, without looking up, he walked toward the long hallway connecting to the back of the office. With each step, his tail waved left to right in frenzied excitement. J.D. grabbed the keys to the campus golf cart and allowed his dog to lead the way down the labyrinth of halls leading to the utility shed. By the time J.D. pulled open the large aluminum garage door, Roscoe was in the passenger side of the golf cart, ready to ride.

They'd see a lot today, as crowds arrived for the annual Latino Festival.

J.D. cranked the engine and off they went. Roscoe enjoyed having a chauffeur for his usual rounds across campus. They zoomed past the cafeteria, decorated for this special day in streamers and balloons. As they passed the picnic seating outside, J.D. slowed down to feed a treat to Roscoe. The Lab lapped up another treat near the student center, which featured a giant bounce house out front. When the pair drove by the softball field, J.D. handed over another treat as he admired the ribbons of every color woven into the metal fences. This was a special day at North Star Community Center.

By the main entrance to campus, just next to the security station, J.D. put his foot on the brake pedal, turned to his dog, and opened his hand with the biggest fistful of treats he could offer. Instead of gobbling them up, Roscoe darted out of the golf cart and ran toward the highway.

Bark! Bark, Bark! Bark!

"Roscoe!"

The Lab galloped on the freshly cut June grass, almost taking down a set of colorful yellow, orange, and green decorations lining the drive. His sharp senses identified something in the distance, farther away than J.D. could see or hear.

Bark! Bark!

"What do you see, boy?"

Roscoe sat on high alert as Darrell, the campus groundskeeper, stepped out of the security booth.

"That dog can hear a steak drop two towns over," he said.

"Hey, Darrell."

"Hey, J.D. Happy festival day!"

"It's my favorite Saturday of the year! Looks like Roscoe is excited about it, too."

"Give it about ninety seconds. You'll notice someone turn in here. I see him do this every day. Well, on the days when a strange car comes around. He's our watchdog."

"I thought that was your job!" J.D. laughed.

Bark! Bark!

"There he goes. He's locked in on something now."

"Darrell, what did you mean by strange car?"

"I just mean one he doesn't recognize. Roscoe knows every car on campus. The workers. The volunteers. The ball players. He even knows the people who drop in to use the free Wi-Fi. He remembers everybody. Give it a minute, you'll see. I know that bark. Someone he's never met is coming this way."

They stood watching until, just as predicted, a food truck barreled down the street. Roscoe darted toward it, running close to the giant tires.

"Roscoe! Come here, boy! Stay back!"

He followed the truck all the way to the back lot by the library. The Lab circled the colorful RV painted with the words "Sand Mountain Street Tacos" in large squiggly letters on the side. It was the first of many vendors arriving for the Latino Festival. J.D. and his team launched the celebration years ago to show the growing migrant population that anyone new to town was welcome at the center. The all-day event honored cultural customs and traditions that the new residents added to the mountainside community. What began as a burrito truck with a mariachi band grew into the largest festival of its kind in the state. As each new vendor set up shop, Roscoe repeated the same energetic chase and welcomed them with his signature slobbery smile.

"I think this is going to be Roscoe's favorite day of the year, too," said J.D.

Over the next hour, the campus transformed into a swirling, twirling dream. Colorful streamers draped down from the streetlamps and shimmered in the breeze. Flags from Hispanic nations adorned buildings, alongside a special community center banner embroidered with their mustang mascot prominently featured. Patty, Brenda, and the rest of the team took great care to set the scene with vibrant decorations. Members of the local Hispanic community did the rest. Red and green tents popped up on the lawn, each stocked with hand-woven fabrics, artisan jewelry, and a sampling of international delicacies people in Rainsville usually needed a passport to peruse. The maintenance crew raised a small wooden stage with large speakers blasting a soundtrack guaranteed to keep all who attended dancing through the deepest siesta. Flamenco dancers posed and dipped in their purple and red frilly dresses, followed by a drum circle that transformed into a Mexican poetry reading mid-way through the beats.

The event drew visitors from Fort Payne to Scottsboro. They came from all walks of life; it was a sight that would have been unrecognizable to a past generation of community members who grew up during the tumultuous pre-Civil Rights Era. This was not their grandparents' community festival.

Ever since J.D. studied sociology at the University of Texas, other cultures fascinated him. He never retired from learning and, after he reconnected with Arley this summer, he wanted to hear more about how she enjoyed attending his alma mater. When he spotted her volunteering at the face painting booth, he took a break from working the crowd.

"Hey Arley, how's the booth going?"

She held up her paint-coated hands, "Does this give you any idea? We've been busy. I'm not sure what's more popular, the sugar skulls or the mustang."

"I'm glad to hear it! Especially since," he lowered his voice, "there's a surprise coming. You may get a few more requests for mustangs before the day ends."

Before Arley could ask for a hint, another voice cut across the celebration.

"¿Por qué puedo tomar clases de español?" Emma asked slowly, failing to form the sentence she wanted. She was in line at the table next to Arley's. There, they recruited students to take Spanish lessons at the community center over the summer.

"There are many reasons to do this," explained the translator. "For starters, to speak to your fellow community members in their native language!"

"Si!" Emma shouted, over-eagerly, "But...Por qué can I take those lessons? Sign me up!"

"I think you mean "Cuando puedo tomar clases de español, Emma," Arley said gently. "You want to ask when, not why."

"Arley! I didn't see you. Will you be my teacher?" Emma said as she rushed over to give her a hug. They'd grown close since Arley started visiting Poppy at the clinic. "No offense, profesora, I'm sure your lessons are tre bien."

"That's French! I think you mean muy bueno!"

The vendor smiled and looked away, shaking her head at Emma's bilingual naïveté.

"I'll be happy to teach you anything, Emma. But I must warn you—my dad's from Mexico and my mom's from Mississippi. That means I speak Spanish with a side of southern. I wish I could get rid of this accent. Mom says my southern drawl makes me sound like a nitwit."

"I love your accent, Arley! It's like you speak in cursive."

"I don't know. I think they have a point. People hear me talk and assume I'm not the sharpest pencil in the bin."

"People assume a lot of things about me, too. That doesn't make them true," Emma added.

"J.D., maybe the community center could offer a language class on how to lose your southern accent? I'd sign up for that one."

He smiled and stepped close to them, as though he was about to share something they should take to heart.

"People worry so much about how they look and sound to others," he said. "When it comes to a southern accent, I say just forget it and be you. If someone thinks you're less than the best for the way you talk, you'll surprise them even more when you show just how spectacular you are. Prove them wrong by being you, cursive talk and all."

"J.D., can I ask you something sort of personal?" Arley questioned. "You just seem to know things other people don't think about."

"Thank you, Arley. That's quite the compliment."

"Why did you leave Texas after graduation? You came back home when you could have gone anywhere."

"The university offered me a teaching job in Austin, you know. Full-time professor."

"But you came back here? No offense. I just always wondered, what happened? I mean, the tacos and live music are enough to stay...but you had a job there, too!"

"This is home. The way I saw it, I had a choice: I could stay there and write about things other people had done. Or I could come back here and do things other people may write about."

Lick. Lick. Thump. Thump. Thump.

Roscoe interrupted with his version of a wet kiss, as he licked J.D.'s hand and sniffed out the potential for more treats. His tail wagged against Arley's leg. Instinctively, she squatted down to his eye level to say hello. His handsome face and bright brown eyes glowed from all the attention of the day.

"You know this is the most famous dog in three counties, right J.D.?" Emma asked. "Every newspaper and social media group I follow has mentioned him in the past few weeks."

"He caused quite a stir, didn't he? I learned a useful lesson," he paused. "If I want to get a lot of press for one of my presentations, I need to arrange an appearance with Roscoe!"

"Do you follow his social media page?" Arley asked.

"Do I? I like every post," Emma said. "I bet half the crowd here liked the picture of him with the mariachi band this morning. Charles and I need to get him to do an ad for our clinic! I think he's even more known than Poppy these days!"

"Get your cameras ready for later," J.D. said. "There's a surprise coming at one o'clock, and I think it will even shock ol' Roscoe!"

With a devilish glimmer in his eye, he darted away to prepare.

By noon, most of the revelers were gathered along Food Truck Row, which stretched in a half-circle around the main stage. A giant, red velvet curtain, hung just for the day, covered the doors of the garage, creating the perfect hiding place for J.D.'s surprise. It was almost time. The plan, which he'd dreamed up with help from Lynde, was for him to tug on a gold braided cord that would split open the curtain just enough for the special guest to step out on stage. Then he'd pull another rope to lower half a dozen piñatas filled with treats.

As Emma and Arley waited for the surprise over queso, something seemed off. Arley kept checking her phone.

"Where are they?" Emma asked.

"Huh?"

"You look like you're all cheese dip with no chips and need someone to bring you a fresh basket. Whose text are you waiting for?"

Arley blushed and looked away.

"Look, it's okay. Whoever you want to see, if you like them...well, I will, too."

"No, it's not that. It's...I thought my mom and dad were going to meet me here. I wanted to show them my booth."

"Think they are alright?"

"My mom is probably worried her tamales don't taste as good as the ones here and decided to stay home. I don't know why they always promise to show up and then bail."

"I know that pain—the phantom limb of abandonment rearing its head. It hurts! Until it doesn't."

"Who abandoned you? Are you and Charles—"

"Oh, even after the nonsense I've put him through, that man don't believe fat meat's greasy! He's not going anywhere."

"Wait, what does that mean?!" Arley laughed.

"It means he's learned the hard way that I can be—" she paused. "I can be a character. He's seen me come apart and he stuck around. That's the kind of person we all should be so lucky to have in our corner."

Arley smiled.

"Just as a good friend," Emma clarified. "He's working at the clinic today, so I'm all by my lonesome. Sia's at camp all summer, so I'm really a solo act."

"Must be quite a camp!"

"Oh, Sia is working it. Literally. It's their first job...camp counselor! I'm so proud! But also...I'm so alone! I'm missing my baby, something fierce. Will you stick with me for the festival? You can be my bonus child today. We can hang out until you figure out what your mom and dad are up to."

Arley slid her cell phone back in her pocket and dipped her tortilla chip deep into the hot queso. With the crowd feasting on burritos, empanadas, and churros, J.D. seized the moment for his surprise. Microphone in hand, he stepped on stage and called the audience to attention.

"We're here today because this is a place where everyone belongs. Maybe you've lived between the mountains your entire life, or maybe you just moved here. Some of us think we talk funny. Others may think I talk funny. It doesn't matter how you sound, what matters is that we're all talking to one another. Everyone is welcome here. To thank you all for making this year's festival one to remember, I want to share a surprise. Drumroll, please!!"

Rat-a-tatta-tatta-tatta-tatta.

"Presenting...the official mascot of North Star Community Center..."

J.D. pulled the golden cord, slowly opening the curtain behind him.

"Introducing...."

Rat-a-tatta-tatta-tatta-tatta

"Trooper the mustang!"

From behind the curtain, he appeared: a fifteen-hand high mustang, or five feet tall as those not familiar with Sand Mountain equestrian culture may describe it. Patty held tightly to his rein and led him on the stage as she walked beside the majestic creature. Bell stood on the other side and soothed the giant animal, stroking his neck as they joined J.D. on stage. North Star Community Center flags, with Trooper's silhouette printed in the insignia, flapped in a gust of wind as though the horse's appearance brought them to life. The crowd stared in awe, then cheered as the beautiful creature gazed out over campus. Fueled by the energy of the applause, Patty's granddaughter, Anna, ran in circles and screamed with excitement. She leapt on the stage and galloped toward the animal.

"I love him! I love him!" Anna shouted, her arms wide open.

The crowd laughed.

"Can I have the first ride, J.D.?"

"Oh, this horse isn't for riding." J.D. said in the mic, "But I would like to invite all children to step up close to the stage. Come on!"

One by one, a group of about two dozen kids weaved their way up to the side of the platform.

"We're going to walk Trooper around campus so he can enjoy the green space. While he takes his lap, you're all invited to take part in a very special tradition. We call it the smashing of the piñatas! And there are plenty to go around. Look up!"

Hanging high over Trooper the mustang were six colorful piñatas, each decorated as ornately as the birthday cakes sold at Variety Bake Shop on the town square.

"Let's count down together. When we get to one, you can start swinging! Are you ready?"

The crowd cheered and whistled. As J.D. reached for the rope to lower the six piñatas, Patty looked over at him with a panicked expression in her eyes.

"J.D." she whispered, "This horse isn't moving."

It was too late to pause. The countdown had begun.

"10...9...8..."

Bell tried coaxing the horse, whispering up toward its ear to "just take one step at a time."

"7...6...5..."

Patty took a more direct approach.

"Move your butt, Trooper—unless you want half the kids in Jackson and DeKalb Counties climbing up for a ride!!"

"4...3...2..."

In unison, the crowd cheered a triumphant "one!" But the horse was already out of the barn, as they say, and Trooper still wasn't budging. J.D. looked up nervously at the rope, reluctant to tug it with the mustang still on stage. Unable to wait a second longer, Anna jumped up to grab it from J.D.'s hand and pulled hard. However, instead of six falling piñatas, a large canvas banner unfurled. This wasn't the plan at all. The heavy canvas flapped downward and revealed four words, spray painted in red.

The banner said: *You're not welcome here.*

The crowd gasped as J.D.'s heart sank.

"My God," he said just before he rushed to pull down the canvas banner, but someone secured it too tightly from the metal rafters. It was stuck. J.D. could hear the commotion of the audience questioning the message in both Spanish and English. He felt the unity of this day sliced by a banner of hate. Some people in the crowd booed while others looked hurt and embarrassed. J.D. pulled harder on the rope, throwing all his body weight into it until, finally, the banner came crashing from above. The sudden reversal of tension sent J.D. plummeting to the wooden stage with a thud; the mustang reared on its hind legs with its hooves lifted. It looked every bit like a mustang about to charge.

Patty's eyes bulged as the reins slipped through her hands. Bell raced toward J.D., while Anna hid underneath the wooden stairs leading up to the platform. The crowd panicked; food truck vendors shut their windows while the band grabbed their instruments and scampered away from the stage. Only one creature moved toward the commotion—Roscoe.

The old Lab seemed unphased by the chaos. He stepped steadily up the stairs, and onto the stage. People noticed, as whispers of "*Look! The dog is going up there,*" danced across the audience. They watched with anticipation, which somehow slowed down the panic. A dog's best magic trick is how quickly it calms a human. People began recording cell phone videos and Paige, who operated Roscoe's social media account, started a live feed of the dog confronting the danger. He stepped closer and closer until the mustang's large, brown eyes connected with the Lab's dark eyes and slobbery smile. The dog stood a mere foot away from the giant horse.

Roscoe lowered his head and stretched his front legs down into a bow. After holding for a beat,

Roscoe lifted himself back on all fours and slowly tilted his neck up at the mustang as though he wanted to give him a wet kiss. The horse bent down and, for just a moment, these two creatures touched noses, connecting despite their differences. In that instant, Patty slipped behind the horse to lift its reins off the ground. She regained control, holding her right hand in the air in victory like a rodeo star. The crowd clapped and cheered, but J.D. still felt uneasy. He had to say something about the hateful banner, but what? As he picked the mic up from the wooden floor of the stage, Roscoe walked to his side. With his dog next to him, J.D. knew what to do.

"Earlier today, I said that no matter our differences, we're all one. Some people may challenge that and have the audacity to claim that's not true. Some may even try to scare you into thinking you're not welcome by writing things on a banner. But let this connection of canine and equine prove to each of us that no matter what we face, we can find common ground—together. Roscoe and Trooper are living proof of that."

"We love you, J.D.!" Emma screamed from the front row. "¡Te queremos!"

As the crowd cheered and the mariachi music resumed, Emma scouted the crowd to investigate who caused the disruption. She figured Xavier was behind the banner attack, and she wanted to be the one to prove it.

By sundown, video of the cross-species connection went viral online. Over 400,000 people viewed the live feed on Roscoe's social media page. Dozens of photos of the "dog and horse kiss," as many described it, were being shared, too. No one talked about the banner. Instead, everyone focused on the unusual connection between the two animals.

Patty, Bell, and J.D. sat in his office, munching on a leftover quesadilla platter. With his belly full, Roscoe stretched out on his dog bed next to J.D.'s desk and fell into a deep sleep. J.D., on the other hand, couldn't stop tapping his leg as he stared out the window. Even though the festival had been deemed a great success, Bell and Patty could sense J.D.'s distraction. They knew he'd stay that way until he figured out who was behind the banner sabotage.

"I've been thinking," Patty said, "You better find the funding for the Roscoe statue you promised. That dog is more popular than ever."

"I never promised a Roscoe statue, Patty. It was a mustang statue," He paused. "But I sure like the sound of a Roscoe statue."

"You're going to have to do it. There's something about that dog. He always becomes the headline. The good headline. Even on a day like today."

"A good headline, for a good boy," Bell said, taking a sip from her Diet Coke can. "You'll raise that money."

Click. Snap. Fizz.

Patty popped open a Coke then asked, "Don't you have a rainy-day fund or something?"

J.D.'s eyes locked on the fizzing carbonation rising from the metal ring on the can as his next big idea bubbled to the surface. He asked, "Where did you two get those drinks?"

"The vending machine in the cafeteria. I sent Arley down to get a few of them for us before she left with Emma," said Patty.

"You know, we sell a lot in those vending machines. Cokes, Doritos, Snickers bars, Cheetos. It adds up more than you think."

"What do you do with the money?" Patty asked.

"It goes back to the community center. It's earmarked for us to spend however we see fit as long as everyone benefits. I like to save it for when we really need it. We haven't spent a dime of it in years."

"Am I thinking what you're thinking, J.D.? Are you going to make it rain?"

"Patty, we're going to count our quarters. That may be enough to bring that statue to life."

"A statue paid for in quarters. I can't tell if you're brilliant or thrifty!" Patty teased.

"He's both," Bell smiled.

CHAPTER 7

The Investigation

"I don't see it," Arley said, as she stared intently at the scraps of paper spread out over the wall like a prize quilt on display at the Jackson County Fair. Each piece was scotch taped to another, with color-coded post-its stuck on top of maps and photographs. The evidence, as Emma called it, coated the room in theories about how the mysterious banner drop at the Latino Festival connected with Roscoe's attack. Emma's investigation didn't search for who did it; she already blamed her ex, Xavier. What stumped her was how he could get away with it without anyone knowing—especially her. She wanted answers.

"Look closer, Arley. There's always a pattern to these things," Emma said as she stretched a red twine string from a photo of the banner to a map of North Star Community Center. She pinned the end of the twine on the corner where Arley found red agate rocks after Roscoe was shot.

"I see nothing," Arley said. "It's just a lot of nothing taped together."

She'd stopped by the vet clinic to browse Emma's rock store, but reluctantly found herself recruited as a co-investigator.

"It isn't anything until it is," Emma said. "It isn't anything…. until you notice. I just haven't cracked it yet."

Emma darted around the room like a hummingbird. Her body was filled with nervous energy as she searched for proof that would confirm what her gut already knew.

"What will you do if you find out it was Xavier?"

"Well, I'd share that info with J.D. Surely he'd ban him from the community center and alert the authorities."

"Alert them to what?" Arley asked.

"That banner was a hate crime, Arley! It told hundreds of people they aren't welcome around here."

"I dunno. That seems a little harsh. It may have just been a prank though, right? A bad joke?"

"Some people shouldn't try to be funny! A joke about intolerance is a nasty laugh. It chips away at the community we've built around here."

Emma pulled back a stool and leaned against the seat, her first break from pacing in an hour. She dangled one foot in the air and kept one foot on the ground, ready to spring back into action if she noticed a new clue. Emma let out a deep breath as she dabbed her fingertips against her face, bouncing her index finger on a spiral curl twisting down her forehead. All the energy she swirled around the room moved into that one finger.

"I'm just so tired," Emma sighed. Her eyes closed as she kept tapping different spots on her cheek and jaw.

"I'm tired, too," Arley whispered.

She pulled out her cell phone and slumped down to stare at the blank screen. No messages. She fiddled with her phone for a few more minutes and when she looked up, Emma's position had changed. Her neck stretched behind her shoulders and her head tilted upward. Emma's spine curved in a half moon formation as her body arched down to her legs, feet firmly planted on the ground. The hummingbird had transformed into a swan. Her silhouette reminded Arley of a ballet dancer stretching, as Emma's eyes remained closed and her hands tap, tap, tapped on her face. She appeared to be doing some type of routine.

Tap. Tap. Breathe. Tap. Tap. Breathe.

Arley awkwardly stared at her friend, unsure if she should leave the room or ask Emma if she was okay. Instead of doing either, she looked back down at the glowing screen in her palm and zoned out on her phone.

Swipe. Swipe. Click.

Arley scrolled through her feed: dog videos and photos of her college friends on summer vacation. In the month since she returned home, her life in Austin seemed a world away, and Arley felt stuck between the Alabama girl she used to be and the college freshman persona she'd tried on for the past year. Neither felt exactly right. She clicked past pictures of friends tubing on the San Marcos River, and photos of a road trip to San Antonio. She almost hit the like button beneath her roommate's selfie at the Riverwalk, but the voice in her head told her *"Don't be too clingy."* Arley never shared anything on her own account either. She just scrolled. She wanted to connect but found it easier to say nothing than to tell anyone how she felt.

Tap. Tap. Tap.

After a few more reps of tapping and breathing, Emma curved her body back up into a standing position, hips wide in a power pose, and let out one gigantically deep breath.

"Ahhhhhhh!"

She looked as though she'd flushed out the frenetic energy that had consumed her earlier, at least for the moment.

"Now, where were we?" Emma asked, staring back at the wall. "Oh, yes. The map."

Arley slid her phone down to her side.

"Actually," Emma said as she squared her shoulders toward Arley, "I was about to ask you why a 19-year-old is so tired."

"What do you mean?"

"I heard you say it."

"Um, I—I don't know."

"I think it has something to do with whatever is always going on in that phone of yours. Here, give it to me."

As Emma reached over to yank the phone from her hand, Arley clenched it harder and hid it behind her back.

"Trust me, child. Set your phone down over there on the counter, at least ten feet away. Disconnect for a minute. Then, follow my lead."

Tap. Tap. Tap. Breathe. Breathe.

Emma dabbed her index fingers over her temples this time.

Tap. Tap. Tap. Breathe. Breathe.

Arley followed along in an unconventional game of *Simon Says*.

Tap. Tap. Tap. Breathe. Breathe.

"Deeper, Arley. Let all that tension out. It's just you and the universe."

Tap. Tap. Tap. Breathe. Breathe.

They continued the routine until Arley's shoulders eased and her clenched jaw relaxed.

"Charles taught me that," Emma revealed. "It's like meditation, but for people who can't let their mind sit still for too long. The tapping helps keep you focused on the now."

"*That* was meditation?"

"A form of it. I can't get to fifteen minutes, but last week it I did ten. And when I started, I could only sit still for a minute or two. You get better at it. It washes away all the dark and twisty thoughts."

"I feel better, sort of refreshed. It's like a hot bath...for my brain."

"Good! That's the point! Although I never understood how a bath could make anyone feel fresh. You're just sitting there in your own dirty water. But, if it's working, keep tapping!"

Ding. Ding.

Arley's phone chimed from across the room. Emma watched her shoulders clenched upwards again—the sound triggered her. Arley darted across the room to grab the device. The Zen got flushed away with a text message.

"What is going on in that phone?"

"Huh? Oh, nothing."

"I see it all over your face, and it's not good. Just tell me. I can probably help."

"It's my mom. Since I came home this summer, I just feel like everything I do is wrong," Arley said. Her eyes fixated on the glowing screen as she scrolled back to text message after text message from her mother.

"Say more," Emma commanded.

"Like today. She wanted me to stay home with her, but she picked up an extra shift at work. So, I came here. Now, she's home and texting me wondering where I am."

"Let me guess, you feel she's controlling you?"

"It's more like I'm her pet. When she wants me around, she wants me around. When she's busy, she wants me in a cage somewhere waiting for her. Just like that pet rabbit she bought."

"I see," Emma said, her eyes glanced over at the wall full of papers and maps, then darted back to Arley. "And how does that make you feel?"

"Like she owns me."

"Oh, Arley. Be careful with words like that. People can't own people."

"It's how I feel. Like I'm her property."

"Have you told her that?"

"What? No, of course not. How could I?"

"Because if it's how you feel, tell her. Don't keep information like that from someone who loves you. Give her the chance to do better."

"It's not that easy."

Emma kept chatting as she moved the red twine from the community center map over to a picture of the clinic. She crossed the line from there to the spot Roscoe was shot with a bb and the main stage of the Latino Festival.

"Can I be real with you? Because in case you forgot, I'm a mother. And if you can believe it, I once had a mother, too."

Arley's eyes widened.

"Say more?" Arley asked.

"Some mamas want us to live the way they lived when they were growing up, but the times have changed—the same rules don't apply now. She may be trying to figure out how to live with her college-aged daughter and all the new rules that come with that. When you left home you had never been on your own before. That's different now. She may text you five times, and it might not be because she wants control. She's probably just checking to see if you've fallen off the side of the Langston Gap Road on her watch. Be glad she knows how to text. Your phone could ring all the time!"

"If she cared that much, she'd be around this summer."

"You mean she'd quit her job and stay at home with you all day? Would you like that? Would she serve you every meal, too?"

"Of course not, she should live her life. But...she and my dad were at a party when I got to town. It's like they forgot about me even coming home. It would be nice to be wanted."

"Of course, baby girl. We all want that," Emma's tone softened as she brushed her hand behind Arley's auburn hair and stroked her back. "Most mamas feel a great deal of pressure to be the perfect example for their daughters. They need to show them how to work hard, but also how to relax. They need to give their babies space, but also make sure they're supported. It's impossible."

As Emma looked at Arley, her eyes landed on the crooked rainbow pin attached to her lapel. She adjusted the pin until it sat perfectly upright.

"Is there something you want to tell your mama? Maybe something about your life in Texas?"

Arley's face turned flushed, then she went pale. She pulled her long hair over her shoulder so it covered the rainbow pin.

"Not really."

"Mamas want to say the right thing to their children, even when they don't know what it is that they should say. Do you think a mama like me hasn't gotten it wrong before?"

"I wish you were my mom," Arley said.

"Don't they all!" Emma smiled, patting her hand behind her head with a wink. "But I mess up all the time. When Sia changed her pronouns, we went through it. I just couldn't get it right. Why is *they* so much harder to remember than *she*?"

"It's not," Arley countered.

"It's not," Emma agreed. "I didn't see that at first."

Arley looked unsure what to say, but Emma didn't give her a chance to respond, anyway.

"Some things aren't hard to remember, but they are hard to change. Even when we want to. Mamas know when they get it wrong, trust me on that one. And it keeps them up at night."

"She makes it pretty clear I'm the one getting it all wrong."

"You? No, I'd be so proud if you were my daughter, Arley. You're wise beyond your years, you're thoughtful and most of all, you are kind."

Arley stared down at the floor. Criticism was easier to hear than compliments.

"Thank you," she whispered. "But I don't see myself like that. I know my mother doesn't."

"There is a lot of pressure to live up to our mama's example. Don't forget, I'm a daughter, too."

"What do you mean?"

"My mama was the best there was. I'd give anything to still have her. Her name was Frances. She grew up mostly without a mother herself, and I'm not sure where she learned to be so wonderful. I still don't think I'm living up to all she was to our family, but I try every day."

"What would she tell me if she were here today?"

"Probably get up and go home, Arley! She'd tell me that when I'd fall asleep at her house after a visit."

"Well, I like it here."

"I like *you* here. But don't let me keep you from your mama. Now get up and go home!"

Arley agreed she'd try an afternoon at home, and Emma turned back to her board of maps and clues, with her brow wrinkled in thought. All the theories that danced around in Emma's head had materialized into physical form on that wall. From the multi-colored post-it notes to the red strings that tied it all together, she'd found order to the madness with it all on display. As Arley took in the amateur sleuth in action, she noticed something missing from the investigation.

"I think there may be one more question to ask," Arley said.

"Oh, I've asked them all," Emma countered. "Just like they do on those mystery podcasts. I've asked Who? What? When? Where? And how?"

"But you haven't asked *why*," Arley said, as she walked toward the door of the clinic break room. "Maybe that's where you'll find what you're looking for."

Emma threw a side eye sharp enough to cut a strand of red twine. She didn't like to be accused of missing something.

"Child, get out of here! Why do Southern people never know how to just leave. We all stick around saying stuff we have no business saying."

"I have just one more thing to tell you," Arley said. "I think Frances would be so proud of you."

"Now *that*, you can say," Emma smiled. "See you later, Arley! Get up and go!"

After Arley left the clinic, Emma combed over the board, and she pulled out another piece of twine. This one was green.

"Why?" she said to herself. "Let's figure this out, Emma."

CHAPTER 8

The Hottest Day

Click. Click. Click.

With a keystroke, J.D. signed the deal. The lone witness to this celebratory moment sat at his feet, tail wagging beneath the desk. Even Roscoe seemed to smile as J.D. hit send.

"We did it, boy!"

Thump. Thump. Thump. Thump.

Roscoe's tail bounced on the carpet like he was clapping for J.D.'s accomplishment. Maybe the dog noticed how hard he'd been working. J.D. had spent weeks analyzing accounting ledgers, calculating cost estimates, consulting artists, and researching metals. This was more than a work project to him; commissioning a one-of-a-kind statue was a dream come true. J.D. got the idea on a trip out West, where he marveled at the craftsmanship of nature-inspired artwork. Indigenous sculpture artists honored great creatures of the plains, including horses and steer, bighorn sheep, and bison. Their craft of molding and shaping metals into animal form captured their power and pureness. The heavy bronze material reflected the animal spirit and preserved its primal prowess for the ages; in turn, these animals become eternally inspiring and, in a way, immortal.

J.D. wanted his community to have their own public art with a similar connection. In the entire three-county region, the only existing statues were a tribute to the band *Alabama*, which featured life-size replicas of the Fort Payne boys who became country music superstars, and a bust of Andrew Jackson which made the list of "the South's most awkward statues" for its "pencil-headed design."

A statue of quality is difficult to construct and, therefore, very expensive. Dime by dime, J.D. found a way to pay for his with money already in the bank. For years his team saved every cent from the community center's vending machine fund. Money earned from selling Cheetos and Funyuns, Snickers bars and KitKats all went into savings with the faith that they'd know the right project when they saw it. There was one spending requirement: the money must be used in a way that benefitted the community. J.D.'s pitch assured Commissioner Bankston that this unique form of artwork would qualify. Including the campus dog in the design added a layer of localism, but it also left J.D. a little nervous. He couldn't have this statue appearing on any "most awkward" lists, so the execution needed to be perfect. He crafted the proposal, ran it by his "squad" of trusted advisors, and sent the plan to the commissioner for review. J.D. felt confident that the final outline was perfect. It featured the mustang mascot *and* Roscoe, in a combination that rivaled chocolate and peanut butter. Barbara came up with the idea to include both animals, then sketched out a beautiful design. Not even the artists in Santa Fe had sculpted a stray Labrador Retriever, but they hadn't met a dog like Roscoe, either. There in his office, with Roscoe sitting beside him, the commissioner's approval came back to J.D. within minutes of its submission.

"You're going to be even more famous now, ol' boy!"

Roscoe smiled. His slobbery tongue dripped as he panted in the summer heat. J.D. slid the water bowl closer to his dog bed, but the Lab didn't want that. He preferred to drink from the giant fountain outside. As he swaggered across the office toward the exit of the administration building, J.D. reluctantly stopped him.

"No, Roscoe. It's too hot out there for you today."

Plop. Plop.

J.D. added a couple of ice cubes to the dog's bowl. Maybe chilled water could entice him away from the splashing ripples of the outdoor fountain.

As Roscoe lapped up a few sips, J.D. leaned back in his desk chair and stared out of the window. Something about the green grass, the midday sunlight, and the faint sound of the softball field loudspeaker transported him fifty years into the past.

In a mint green house on West Street, a few blocks from the town square, J.D. grew up in the epicenter of adventure. It seemed like millions of neighborhood kids lived around him, and they convened every afternoon as pirates, basketball and baseball players, race car drivers, and rodeo stars. Once, they even attempted to dig a makeshift swimming pool in his backyard. That effort ended when a kid got hit in the head with a pitchfork. As J.D. told the tale, *"He bled some, but was okay."* These were good kids having a good time, and in moments of tranquility between launching new projects and running the community center, J.D. traveled back there with them in his mind. To his happy place.

On his shelf of mementos sat a tattered old football. The seams barely held it together, but the pigskin was as valuable to him as if it was from the winning touchdown of a national championship. A square, faded photograph in a vintage frame leaned against the football. The frame broke years ago, but the ball holds it up, the same way ball held together the dozen friends in the picture. They'd gathered for the snapshot after the famous East-West football game. In the center of the group, twelve-year-old J.D. wrapped his arms around a shaggy stray he called Shy Dog—his first pet, even if he never truly domesticated the nomadic stray.

The photograph documented friendships that began in the backyard sandbox at his parents' home. J.D. would watch the neighborhood kids throwing baseballs in the vacant lot. They all knew his older sister, Carolyn, full of charm and grace. He was the kid brother until, one day, his neighbor Doug said, "Come on over, we need an extra player." From there, the neighborhood became a training ground for his future high school football glory. J.D. learned how to be a quarterback, but also a diplomat and community organizer. He'd break up squabbles before they rose to a level of a fight and disarm tense situations with wit or logic. However, his legacy was born when he organized the East-West football game with the kids across town. They still talk about that game at his high school reunions, with much debate over who actually won the mash up.

J.D. smiled as he stared at the photograph, his young arm holding tightly to Shy Dog. That stray taught him the connection between human and dog, even if it was a friendship with an untamable canine companion. Young J.D. tried and tried to convince the dog to stay at his house at night. He lured him with scraps from his dinners, piled blankets in the garage for a make-shift bed, and one day even dragged him inside. The dog always ran away, unless J.D. was throwing a ball. When J.D. and his friends tossed around the football, the dog stuck around. After the final play of each game, Shy Dog moved on to his next adventure down the road.

Thump. Dredge! Thump.

Roscoe pushed his water bowl across the room, his old body struggling to bend so low to the ground. The sound pulled J.D. back into the present.

"Need some help, old boy?"

J.D. sat his water bowl on a pile of books so Roscoe wouldn't have to lean over as much. The dog took a few drinks, then looked up at his person before gazing at the front door again.

"You really want out, don't you? Well...okay. Who am I to lock you up?"

As J.D. opened the lobby door, Roscoe waddled by him, his back leg still stiff from the bb injury. On his way out, he brushed his body against J.D.'s pants leg. The graze seemed to say, "Thank you."

"Have fun out there! I'll be working on your statue while you enjoy this hot day."

And he did. An hour became two, then three, as J.D. sketched out ideas for where the statue would be placed on campus, which direction it would face, and how to showcase it at night alongside the streetlamps lining the center's walkways. He got lost in sorting through the details that would bring his unconventional idea to life. J.D. concentrated so hard, he didn't feel the sweat building on his brow, or that his damp shirt stuck to his back.

Knock-knock. Knock-knock.

"Bell?"

Knock-knock. Knock-knock.

He recognized the rhythmic double knock he and his wife used to let the other know they were on the other side of the door.

"Come on in!"

Knock-knock. Knock-knock.

She was saying something through the back door to his office, but until he got closer, he couldn't understand she was asking him to unlock it.

"That's so strange," he said as he opened it and hugged her hello. "I know I didn't lock that door. I never do."

"Why are you so...sweaty?"

"Oh, I guess I am. Is it hot in here?"

"Hot as blazes! Turn on the A/C!"

In his deep focus, he hadn't noticed the air conditioning stopped working. The summer heat beamed in through the tall windows in his office. With no air flow, the air inside was like a sauna. As J.D. reached for the phone, he stumbled.

"J.D., are you okay?"

"I think I need some water. Can you find Darrell and check on Roscoe in this heat?"

"Roscoe! What about you, J.D.? I think the heat may have made you sick."

"I'll be fine. I just need a minute to cool off."

Before she could, Patty burst into the office, out of breath and sweating herself.

"It's Roscoe!" she exclaimed. "You both should come quickly. I think he had a heatstroke. I need help moving him!"

J.D. and Patty hurried out to the fountain, where Roscoe laid on his side, his tongue hanging over the side of his mouth and eyes glazed over. His stressed eyes looked right up into the sun. Bell wasn't far behind, carrying a cup full of ice she'd instinctively filled up when she heard the words heatstroke.

"We have to get him out of the sun," Patty said, as a crowd of people gathered around to watch.

"Roscoe? Roscoe, can you hear me?"

The sound of J.D.'s voice seemed to register with the dog.

"Do you think a piece of ice may help?" asked Bell.

"Let a piece melt in his mouth," Patty said.

"We need to move him inside," J.D. determined. "Everyone back up so we can lift him."

More and more people gathered, their faces full of concern.

"Roscoe, hang in there," J.D. said as he reached under the dog's thick belly to raise him from the ground. Instead of letting himself be carried inside, Roscoe jumped onto his feet, wiggled his body as though he needed to shake off water after a swim, then leapt into the campus fountain. The crowd cheered.

"Well, how about that!" Patty yelled. "Back to life!"

"But what on earth just happened?" J.D. asked. "That was...strange."

After the Lab finished his dip in the fountain, J.D., Bell, and Patty led Roscoe back into the office. Bell made an ice pack for J.D. and gently placed it on his shoulders. Both man and dog were back to normal. It was as though they were linked; when one felt bad, the other intuited it.

Once the air conditioner service was restored, the office quickly cooled down. Darrell had discovered that the circuit breaker in the back of the school had been tampered with, causing the A/C throughout the building to fail on a ninety-five-degree day. More concerning, Darrell found a piece of red agate on top of the fuse box where the circuit was flipped. The rock matched the ones Arley found after Roscoe was shot.

"Looks like someone is making a statement," said J.D.

"What are we going to do, J.D.? These incidents are getting out of hand." asked Patty.

"We're locking that fuse box up," J.D. declared.

"Emma's going to want to know about this," Bell warned.

"But what are we going to do—" Patty said, unsatisfied with the previous answer. "What are we going to do about Xavier?"

J.D. stared back at his photo from the East-West game, thinking of the many conflicts his neighborhood kids worked out. He had a big one to solve now.

"Society embraces our lowest possibility. We'll choose the high road. If we can confirm Xavier is behind this, I want a meeting with him. We need to talk."

CHAPTER 9

Fourth of July

Long lines of yellow light stretched across Weatherington Park. Summer shadows left their mark over the green grass that carpeted this gathering spot, from the asphalt edge of the parking lot to the tip of the rocky bluff. Streaks of sunset poured across the lawn and spilled over the granite cliff lookout perched high above the Tennessee River. For decades, this rock bed plateau served as nature's viewing station for Fourth of July parties. Even the bright beams of sunset couldn't compete with the red-white-and-blues decorating picnic tables and people alike, all dressed early for the evening fireworks show.

"Bell, is that what I think it is?" Emma shouted down from the center of the gazebo. Her voice bellowed loudly enough to be heard over the music that blasted from speakers on each side of a rectangular folding table. The center of the table was bare, waiting to be filled with local delicacies for a July Fourth feast.

With a knowing nod, Bell placed two crisp paper boxes from Variety Bake shop on the table. The sides of her lips twirled upwards in a sly grin as she unfolded the flaps and the scent of sugar wafted up from the dessert inside. As she opened the second box, her smile grew wider as she lifted a near-identical delicacy from its container and revealed twin buttercreams, both white cake with vanilla icing, each with a crescent of hand-drawn, frosting flowers on the corner. The cakes were adorned with red and blue blooms, and with small green petals that curved in a floral fireworks display of their own. With one swoop she placed each on the serving pedestal.

"Tastes like tradition!" Bell said, as she licked a small pat of icing from her index finger.

"I knew it!" Emma smiled. She nudged Charles with her elbow. "She'd find a reason to bring a birthday cake to a funeral."

"Are you complaining?" Charles asked, his grin already revealing he knew the answer.

"No one seems to mind when I show up with birthday cake!" said Bell.

"Well, I guess it is America's birthday!" Emma said, leaning into Charles' arm. "Cut me a piece!"

The three friends orchestrated the food table every year, serving dozens of people ahead of the fireworks show. On this holiday there were no strangers at Weatherington Park, at least not by the time the fireworks finished. Many people knew each other only from previous Fourth of July festivities, but tradition runs deep. For most of the crowd, today was the only time they saw each other all year, so they made it count.

Everyone became "Fourth of July family" thanks in part to a potluck extravaganza that started at dusk. Wayne and Mary shared their homemade ice cream in red plastic cups with anyone who wanted a scoop. Sonny served up helpings of Tate's barbeque with a side of Angela Joy's baked beans. Cyndi decorated sugar cookies. The Patrick boys arrived with an arsenal of sparklers and bottle rockets for those who lacked patience for the big show to start. Heather and Jeremy orchestrated an informal pyrotechnics pre-show, setting off enough colorful smoke bombs to coat the park with a magical purple haze. Every year, the crowd mingled as those summer shadows grew longer and the sky turned from blue to orange to navy, when Roman candles competed with twinkling stars. This year's holiday seemed extra special since a full moon rose over the pine trees on the horizon. It glistened across the sky. One could see for miles from the park's overlook, a steep cliff anchored on the side of Sand Mountain. The view stretched all the way to the winding water of the Tennessee River, which snaked from Scottsboro to Guntersville.

"Isn't it beautiful?" Bell sighed, standing alone by Emma and Charles.

"With a moon like that, who needs fireworks!" Emma agreed.

"Oh, I think they do," Bell said, looking over at Anna and Lilah running circles across the lawn. Their grandmother, Patty, stood in the center, like the sun with two wild planets whirling around her. The girls threw snap-its, unleashing high-pitched screams of joy when one of the tiny paper-covered fireworks hit the ground and sparked with a signature pop. Their frenzied game of chase-and-snap took them to the gazebo, which was a little too close to the cliff for Bell's comfort. She tried to distract the girls with the temptation of more desert.

"Want another slice of cake, Anna?"

"I'm tight as a tick!"

"What on Earth?" Emma shot back.

"I said I'm tight as a tick. One more bite of cake and I'll pop," Anna said. "Just like this."

Pop! Pop! Pop-pop!

She threw a handful of snap-its toward Lilah.

"Easy girls. We're grown folks. If you snap at us, we may snap back," warned Emma. "And you don't want to see me pop off!"

"Yes, Ms. Emma," Anna agreed, as she stood a little straighter and turned her attention elsewhere.

With the moon glowing high in the sky, the crowd convened on the overlook by the edge of the bluff. It was a front row view for the fireworks show.

"You coming, Bell?" Emma asked.

"Oh, not yet. I'm hanging back for J.D. He'll be here soon."

"Where is he anyway?"

"He's working on something special with Arley. You'll see. Y'all go on down to the overlook and get ready for the show."

"He's always up to some kind of surprise!"

"We can wait with you," Charles offered.

"It's okay. You two can save us a spot."

"We've got to go, Charles. I can't stand to be in the back row," Emma pushed.

"When the fireworks go off, we are all on the front row," Charles smiled as he wrapped his arm over her shoulder. "Just look up and you're as close as anybody."

"I hate it when he's right!" said Emma, as she linked her arm across his back, walked toward the overlook, side by side with Charles.

Bell smiled as her best friends seemed to have become more to each other than business partners. She thought to herself, *"Maybe they figured out what most of the town has seen between them since they met!"*

While everyone stood shoulder-to-shoulder at the overlook, Bell fluttered around the gazebo like a hummingbird nursing a flower. She boxed up all the leftover food and enjoyed one last nibble of birthday cake. As she stepped down the three wooden stairs to the walkway with leftovers in hand, her foot nearly tripped over a lump on the concrete.

"Ohhh!" she gasped. She froze mid-step just before her sandal touched a red cardinal laying on its side on the walkway.

"Poor little thing!"

The bird laid lifeless with one of its wings outstretched and broken as though it had been a toy for a wild animal, or perhaps flew into something head-on and crashed. Bell's eyes watered, her heart ached for the little bird that died amid the crowd of revelers. Bell used some cardboard from one of the Patricks' boxes of sparklers to scoop up the bird and move it into the woods. She thought the forest was a more fitting place for the bird to be laid to rest, and she hoped none of the children would see it there. Under the light of the full moon, Bell walked back to the gazebo with a heavy heart. A sadness coated her, as did a slight sense of doom. Southern tradition states that a visit from cardinal means a loved one is saying hello from the other side. A dead cardinal on the Fourth of July felt like a bad omen. She looked up and spotted a lone buzzard flying high overhead.

"One's for sorrow," she said to herself, quoting another Southern superstition that many cite as faithfully as a daily horoscope.

"Come on, let me see one more!" She said, looking up. Two buzzards equaled joy. With her head toward the heavens, she didn't notice the figure of a man approaching until she felt a touch on her shoulder.

"Did I miss the fireworks?"

"J.D.!"

"Better late than never," he said. "But I think you're going to love the surprise."

"I'm so glad you're here...more than you could know." Bell glanced over at the forest where she'd placed the dead cardinal. "Where's Roscoe? I thought you were going to bring him?"

"Oh, I left him at the community center. I thought he'd be better off in the A/C on his bed in my office, rather than out here with all the fireworks. The sound is liable to scare him."

"You keep him so safe."

"Looks like everyone is having a great time out there," he said, speaking loudly so they could hear his voice over the music that blasted out from the crowd. "It's about to get even better."

J.D. and Bell watched their "Fourth of July family" glazed in moonlight, all gathered on the lookout. They danced and swayed and celebrated the night by the edge of the cliff. Danger may surround us all, but so does life. Light from the full moon cast a glow over the crowd. And then, something else lit the night sky—something new to the festivities.

Whir. Whir. Whir.

"What is that, Charles?" Emma asked. "That noise sounds like my aunt's old box fan."

Whir. Whirrrr. Whirrrrrrrr.

It grew louder, as if not one but two, six, and then maybe even a dozen box fans blew on high.

"I think it's coming from down there," Emma's eyebrows arched upwards as she nodded her head toward the cliff.

Whirrrrrrrrrrrrrrrr.

Suddenly, the breeze from at least fifty illuminated drones wafted over Emma, Charles, and

Bell as a LED light show flew overhead, launched up from the valley. J.D. smiled as wide as the panoramic landscape. His surprise had arrived. The drones moved in formation with multi-colored lights synced to a soundtrack from the ground.

"We did it, J.D.! The light show is on!" Patty screamed as she turned the music up all the way.

The drones flashed in reds, blues, and whites as they moved higher towards the moon. It looked as if the drones would rocket into the stratosphere until, in an instant, they stopped mid-air and locked in a pattern together in the heavens. Like a life-size puzzle, they flew around to spell out the word "Welcome!" Next, they zoomed into place in the shape of a waving American flag. Then the Statue of Liberty. Next, the drones moved up and down and around as though the whirring machines themselves were fireworks.

"This is wild!" Emma shouted, and the full crowd cheered behind her. "Wild!"

"It ain't over yet, y'all!" Patty said.

"Oh, J.D. This is mesmerizing." Bell grabbed his arm. "I love it! I just love it!"

"Patty and I have been trying to make it happen for years. Arley helped us get it together. She figured out the tech. Look over there," he pointed.

Arley stood at the far side the overlook, just past the crowd, and quietly operated a remote control as big as a pizza box.

"Arley! You're doing great!" Bell called out.

"Wait for it, Bell...the best part is coming up!"

WHIRRRRR.   WHIRRRRRRRRR. WHIRRRRRRRRRR.

The flying illuminated machines flipped and turned. Some flew higher while others dropped quickly toward the bottom of the flock. They were getting in place for something—something special. In a blink, all of their LED lights turned off so that they were invisible in the darkness. When they illuminated again in electric blue and white, the crowd cheered at the shape of two animals sketched out overhead.

"Oh, J.D. He's here after all!" Bell gasped, staring at the dog and mustang lighting up the sky.

"There's ol' Roscoe," J.D. chuckled.

"And Trooper, too!" Bell said. "It's just breathtaking."

The drones maneuvered so that each animal slowly moved closer toward one another until the dog and horse touched noses in the sky. For anyone who had stepped foot on North Star Community

Center's campus just a few weeks earlier, it was a familiar sight.

"They look just like they did at the Latino Festival!" exclaimed Bell. "How did you do that?"

"Our art teacher made the sketch from one of those photos everyone was sharing on social media," J.D. said.

"I should have guessed Barbara drew this. It's so beautiful!"

"Arley scanned her design for us and helped program the drones. She really knows a lot from a STEM program at her college."

"Wow! I am impressed. Her mom must be so proud!"

"Her mom? Is she here?"

"Yes, I saw her down in the crowd."

"Arley will not like that," said J.D. "Something is going on between the two of them. She said her mom thinks she is—what was the word she used? I think she called Arley ordinary."

"Ordinary," Bell repeated. "Well, she needs to look up. Because what Arley helped you create tonight is extraordinary."

Whirrrrrrrrr. Whirrrr. Whirrrr.

The drones slowly descended beneath the overlook, accompanied by a flutter of applause from the crowd, which marked the end of the drone show and the beginning of the fireworks.

Boom! Boom-boom! Flash! Boom!

Arley began packing up the drone remote as the crowd gazed up in awe of the annual fireworks display. From the overlook, they could see all the other fireworks celebrations taking place along the river. The glow of the show at Goosepond illuminated the horizon. Flashes of bottle rockets launched from piers and pastures stretched from Guntersville to Langston to Section. The South Sauty fireworks display sparkled like lace falling from the sky. Over in Weatherington Park, bright reds, purples, and blues exploded from the valley below, creating the illusion that the crowd was inside the fiery festivities.

Arley closed the latches on a box of drone equipment. When she looked up, her mother towered over her.

"Are you responsible for this?" she asked her daughter.

"Mom! I didn't know you were coming."

"We've spent every Fourth of July together since you were born, Arley. Did you think I'd miss this? Or did you think about me at all? I don't recall you asking where your father and I would be tonight."

"Dad is here, too?"

"There!"

Her mother pointed to Arley's father next to the overlook; colorful fireworks reflected on his face. Somehow, the only color to land on her mother's skin was rocket red. With sparks flying high in the sky, she looked down at her daughter as Arley slowly stood, leaving a messy pile of wires and controllers on the ground. They faced each other eye-to-eye, so similar to one another in height and stance, yet at this moment their point of views couldn't have been more different.

"So," Arley said, as she fussed with her long, curly mane, trying to center the part. "What did you think of the show?"

"What did I think of the show? The drones?" her mom replied. She reached over to move Arley's part back to the side and tugged the back of her daughter's shirt to smooth the wrinkles.

"Yes, ma'am. The drones. I programmed the show."

"Everyone is here for the fireworks. We really didn't need that."

"You didn't like it?"

"I didn't say that Arley. I said no one needed that. The fireworks are enough."

Boom! Boom! Ahhh!

Red and blue streams of sparks showered above the crowd in the distance.

"Everyone seemed to like the drones," Arley said. "I wanted to do something special for J.D. after all he's been through this summer."

"What about your father? Did you think to do anything nice for him? Or for me?"

"I...well, it's just—"

Arley stammered, unable to say what she'd thought so many times this summer. She wanted to tell her mother about how hurtful it was when she'd arrived home from college only to be forgotten. She wanted to explain how her mother's passive aggressive suggestions, like leaving clothes out that were *"better for her build,"* made her feel more like an accessory than a daughter. Arley wanted to scream that she'd never come home for the summer again.

All the things she yearned to say were pushed deep down inside her belly, capped by a fear of her mother's reaction. The air smelled burnt as smoke from the fireworks drifted between them, and Arley said nothing at all. Instead, she pretended to be a rock. Just standing there, reacting to nothing, being nothing as her mother's words washed over her without earning a reaction. Over the years, Arley learned pretending to be a lifeless rock was the only way to stop the berating bullets of her mother's criticisms. Today her mother had so many to share.

"You're wasting your talent," she said. "I didn't raise a grown woman to play with flying toys."

Arley slowly breathed in, just as Emma taught her, gently tapping on the side of her own leg. It reminded her she was still human, still worthwhile and, most of all, still herself. Even when she was told *"Maybe you shouldn't have come back here."* Pretending to be a rock was her only power against the verbal attack.

Tap. Tap. Tap.

Clap. Clap. Clap. Clap.

As the crowd applauded the finale of the fireworks show, the cheers drowned out her mother's voice as the stars and bright moon regained control of the horizon. When the clapping stopped, her mother realized strangers may be listening—that always put an end to her narcissistic rants.

"We'll continue this conversation at home," her mother whispered. She disappeared in the crowd as Arley stood alone in the post-fireworks smoke dropping from the sky.

She gathered the drone equipment in slow motion, stunned and numb from the words hurled at her in front of a hundred people, yet witnessed by no one. As Bell and J.D. approached her, Arley did her best to fix her face.

"Arley Flores! You are amazing!" Bell exclaimed.

"Arley, I am so proud of you!" J.D. said as he rushed toward her. "This is an unforgettable night. Especially for me. I never thought I'd see ol' Roscoe and Trooper touch noses like that again."

"And to see it in LED lights! Ah-mazing!" Emma shouted, as she ran up and engulfed Arley in a hug so tight it pushed the air out of her lungs.

Behind her, Charles' arms were full of red solo cups filled to the top with homemade ice cream.

"It's time to celebrate!" he declared.

"Where is your mom and dad, Arley?" Bell asked. "Would they like to join us?"

From Arley's facial reaction, Bell and Emma could discern more than words would convey.

"We'll celebrate with them next time," Bell said.

"Tonight is for you and your people to love on you," added Emma. "You make us so much better."

Buzz. Buzz.

During the ice cream social, J.D. felt his cell phone ringing in his pocket, but his focus was on his crew.

Ding. Ding. Ding.

Next came the texts. First to J.D., then to Bell's phone, too. All their phones began lighting up. Once Emma's group text shared the news, the full squad stood under the moonlight with their faces illuminated by the alarming messages glowing on their screens. In one hand, they held their cups of melting ice cream, in the other they grasped their phones staring down in shock at the news about Roscoe. He wasn't safe within the air-conditioned comforts of J.D.'s office as expected. Instead, Vann found him during his nightly rounds. The dog was lying by the side of the highway, one foot out across the white line on the road, in a patch of grass across from the community center. He appeared to be breathing, but barely, after being hit by a car. The texts kept coming.

Ding. Ding.

Darrell: We moved Roscoe back to your office. I think you'll want to come over to be with him.

J.D.: I'm on the way.

Darrell: He got out because someone unlocked his doggy door outside your office.

Darrell: There's something else you should know. We found this red rock beside the door.

He sent a photo of a single piece of red agate placed on the very top of the plastic frame to the doggy door.

Ding. Ding! Ding! Ding!

On Emma's group chat, news about the famous dog quickly spread across three counties. Already, people started showing up at the community center to help. Most had diverted their drives home from the fireworks show to see if they could help. As J.D., Bell, Charles, and Emma arrived at the community center, they saw a crowd of at least twenty people standing in an unusual glow in the parking lot. Someone had given out leftover sparkles and the crowd was using them as makeshift vigil candles.

No one spoke a word as J.D. walked past. They didn't have to, their faces said, "*We're here for you.*" The black Lab that wandered into J.D.'s life had found a place in the hearts of the entire community, but so had J.D. He paused just before passing through the door to the building.

"Thank you all so much for coming out tonight. There are no better people than those of you living between the mountains. I'll tell ol' Roscoe you are out here sending love," he said.

Bell whispered to J.D., "They came for you, too."

J.D. grabbed her hand and turned back to the crowd.

"I feel the love. Thank you all so much. Now please, go enjoy the holiday with your own families. We'll keep you posted on ol' Roscoe."

One by one, J.D., Bell, Charles, Emma, and Arley walked through the front door to the administration building in a procession toward Roscoe's corduroy bed. As Emma passed beside the doggy door, where Roscoe had escaped during the fireworks, she grabbed the red agate stacked on top of the plastic frame. Her eyes glared as she clenched it tightly in her fist, certain it came from her store. She also knew, deep in her bones, that her ex, Xavier, had placed it there after he unlocked it.

CHAPTER 10

Hit and Caught

Pain feels different for a dog. Scars of the past and worries of the future sit out of mind, like spectators on the roadside while a canine's momentary aches race through his head as fast as cars speeding down Highway 72. For the old, black Labrador Retriever plopped on his side in his corner of J.D.'s office, the thought of the moment was his rear legs. He squirmed and wiggled, lifting his head to adjust his weight so that the pain would ease. While he tried to find a comfortable position, the dog didn't seem to notice the sound of a red rock slam down a few feet away. Emma pounded it on J.D.'s desk in outrage.

"How dare he unlock that door! Xavier has no business even being out here, much less messing with Roscoe," she shouted.

J.D.'s focus remained unflinchingly devoted to his dog. His calm eyes locked with Roscoe, as though they understood each other.

"Now's not the time, Emma," Charles said.

But Emma's focus remained unflinchingly devoted to justice.

"This is on him. If that dog doesn't make it, I'll—"

"Emma, enough. It's not the time."

"There's never a good time for bad news, Charles. I'm going to fix it. I'm going to find that man and make this right," she said. "One way or the other."

Before Charles could respond, Emma slipped out the back door into the dark, humid July night. He chased after her, but it was too late. She'd disappeared. Bell crouched beside Roscoe and filled bowl after bowl with everything she could find, from dry kibble to leftover hot dogs to a scoop of melted ice cream. She lined up at least six bowls beside him to form a canine buffet.

"I don't think he's hungry, Bell," said J.D.

"But eating may help him feel better," she replied. "I want to help him."

J.D. rubbed his hand over Roscoe's forehead, their eyes still locked in their special bond.

"He's bruised, not broken. I can tell," he said. "Isn't that right, ol' boy?"

"Charles," Bell asked, "What's your opinion?"

After an examination, Charles quickly felt convinced Roscoe was only grazed by the car, or maybe it missed him altogether. His injury could also be a strained his leg from leaping out of the way, but the animal was clearly laid back in pain. J.D. gathered materials in his office to create an ice pack out of zip-lock bags and built a soft cushion out of leftover streamers from the Latino Festival to steady Roscoe's leg.

"Y'all going to be here a while?" Charles asked, as J.D. perfectly positioned the padding around the dog's sore rear feet.

"Just a while longer," J.D. said. "Until Roscoe falls asleep."

"I know just the thing for that soreness. I'll get one of our vet techs to bring some medicine up from the clinic. But for now, I have to go look for Emma. I'm worried about her out there on her own."

"Go find her," J.D. said. "Nothing is more dangerous than a violent man."

Roscoe whimpered as Charles left the room, which sent the friends in a frenzy to make him more comfortable.

"Maybe this will help cheer him up," Arley said.

She had found one of Anna's stuffed animals stuck behind the couch cushion in J.D.'s office. It was a solid black Lab, just like Roscoe. The stuffed animal was so realistic, it looked like a living puppy.

"No, not that!" J.D. exclaimed, his eyes opening wide.

But it was too late.

Bark! Bark! Bark!

"What did I do?" Arley asked, as Roscoe sprung up out of his dog bed and began snarling at the stuffed animal.

Bark! Bark!

"Here boy, it's ok. See? Just a toy," she held it out toward him.

This only seemed to make matters worse.

Bark! Bark!

J.D. leapt up quickly to chase after Roscoe, stumbling over the coffee table in the office. His knee took the brunt of the blow and he tumbled to the ground.

"J.D.!" Bell gasped, as she stepped backwards into the half a dozen food bowls she'd laid out for Roscoe. The hotdogs and ice cream squished under her shoes and she fell on her backside, landing a few inches away from J.D.

"Put that stuffed dog away!" J.D. called out from the floor.

"This?" Arley held up the miniature stuffed Roscoe.

Bark! Bark! Grrrrrr!

Roscoe went wild, even with hurt rear legs, as he faced off with what seemed to be his biggest threat: the stuffed dog.

"Ok, ok, Roscoe. I get it!" Arley said, sliding the doppelgänger into J.D.'s desk drawer.

Once the stuffed animal was secured, Roscoe limped back to his bed and plopped back on his side. His head now laid on the padding J.D. designed for his rear legs, but the dog didn't seem to mind the extra pillow. Bell and J.D. helped each other stand. Like Roscoe, they were both bruised, but not broken. In fact, they each had huge smiles on their faces after the outburst.

"I guess he's doing better than we thought," J.D. said, "to attack his mortal enemy like that!"

"I'm so sorry!"

"It's okay, Arley. You couldn't have known he'd react that way. Roscoe has a jealous streak. And it comes out strong with that little stuffed animal! He's territorial!"

"You should see him around a cat!" Bell added.

"That's the main reason we don't take him home with us," J.D. said. "He's a one-dog kind of canine, and with our pets at home, I have a feeling he may go Cujo on them!"

The friends had a good laugh, as Roscoe's tail wagged as though he knew he made them happy. J.D. crouched back down next to his dog as Bell refilled the bowls of food. Arley walked outside, knowing her parents would be expecting her home soon. A small group gathered in the distance, their sparklers replaced with candles. Charles stood by the door, his thick eyebrows tense as his eyes searched for Emma in the crowd.

"Looks like they are holding light for Roscoe," Charles said. "Should we go tell them he'll be alright?"

"Let's leave that to J.D.," Arley said. "Mind if I join you to look for Emma?"

"Sure, Arley."

"Do you think she is okay?"

"I think Emma is Emma."

"It's just," Arley paused. "It's like she has a fire inside that just won't go out. She's always burning hot."

"Say that again, Arley. And think about it."

"Burning hot?"

"No, the first part."

"She has a fire inside that just won't go out."

"That's it," Charles said. "We should all be so lucky."

"She just always seems so—" Arley struggled to find the word.

"I think you're mistaking that fire for passion. Emma cares deeply. She feels deeply, too. More than anyone I ever met. We should all be so lucky to have a fire inside us that burns so hot."

"You say this, even as she's out there chasing after her ex?"

"Lord help him if she finds him," Charles said. "She doesn't need someone to ride in on a horse and save her, but when she wants a soft place to land, I'm here. I have to admit, I'm so scared for her right now."

"You really care for her, don't you?" Arley asked.

"I fell in love with her the first day I saw her looking for Poppy on Langston Road. I fell in love with her again the second day I saw her. And again, on the third."

"We always wanted you two to get together!"

"Me, too! And now that we are, I'm never going anywhere."

"Never is a promise, Charles."

"Never," he echoed. "I promise. You can trust me on that. I wouldn't change a thing about Emma. Especially that fire."

As they neared the candlelit crowd in the parking lot, Arley saw a surprising pair of faces holding vigil and insisted Charles go on searching for Emma without her. When he saw who it was, he understood.

"Mom? Dad? What are you two doing here?"

"Arley! We heard the news," her father said, his voice tender and concerned.

"Everybody loves Roscoe. I've never even met him, and I feel like I know him from all the pictures and stories in the paper," her mom added.

"Well, he's going to be okay. I've been inside with him since the fireworks show."

"Oh, what a relief!" her mother exclaimed, holding her hand over her chest.

The small crowd, made mostly of their church friends, sighed out calls of "Amen" to the good news. Arley's mother was always on her best behavior around her church friends. They thought of her as the mother of the year.

"I'm just sort of surprised you care," Arley said, her shoulders pulled back and spine stretched tall.

She felt empowered at the community center. This was her home turf.

"Of course I care, Arley. I love animals!"

"At the fireworks show you didn't say a word about seeing Roscoe drawn in drone lights."

"That wasn't an animal. That was a hobby. It was lights, not a dog."

Arley just stared, her own fire burning inside her belly.

"What your mother means," Arley's dad explained, "Is that when we saw the text about Roscoe, we had quite a scare. We know you became close to that dog this summer."

"You spend more time with that dog than with either of us!" Her mother snapped at them both.

"Well...you're probably right. And I do care about Roscoe. I care about everybody out here. A good dog knows good people."

"Animals are the best of us," her dad said. "We've learned that since we adopted Bunny."

"I still can't believe you two got a rabbit while I was at school!"

"He's the sweetest thing," her mother said. Her demeanor softened as she talked about the rabbit. "He lets me pet him and rests his head on my chest.

And when I'm feeling stressed or sad, it's like he knows what I'm feeling."

"I get that," Arley said.

She had never even imagined her mom stressed or sad. It was a new side to her mother, who usually was the one making her feel sad or stressed.

"Want a ride home, Arley?" her mother asked. "Bunny will be glad to see you."

"Um...sure," she said cautiously.

With the candlelight extinguished and the red taillights of Arley's parents' car fading down the road, Emma Johnson re-emerged from the night-coated campus. She marched across the community center lawn with the stomp and authority of a jail warden as she directed her helper on where to take her captive.

"Keep an eye on him, Darrell!" Emma shouted behind her. "Trust me, he's a runner."

Darrell walked about twenty feet behind her, with Xavier sandwiched between them. Charles wasn't with them. The fire inside Emma burned hotter than ever, as she led them both to J.D.'s office. She burst through the double doors and called out to the empty entranceway.

"We've got a visitor, J.D. Better keep Roscoe away from this dangerous man," Emma shouted.

She marched him down the small hall lined with J.D.'s collection of photos, posters, and plaques. Emma walked Xavier past J.D.'s office door, where she knew Roscoe was resting, and turned the lights on in the conference room. The large meeting table stretched from wall to wall with enough seats to host twenty guests. To the right was a bookshelf that stretched floor to ceiling. To the left was a banner that read "Best community center in the state." She scanned the room and scouted out where to place him.

"Darrell, sit him over there," Emma pointed to the chair in the center of the room. She stepped aside as Xavier stomped his heavy brown boots on the carpet. He seemed winded, just from a walk, and his pale skin was flushed pink and red around his cheeks.

"I'll sit where I want to sit. You ain't the police," Xavier said, as he wiped his palm across his unkempt beard.

"You don't want to talk like that up here, Xavier. The man I'm about to bring in is powerful. He's going to throw the book at you," she said, turning her head toward the doorway waiting for J.D. to walk inside the conference room.

"You're not the boss of me," Xavier muttered under his bourbon-soaked breath.

"J.D. he's getting sassy back here!" she shouted.

"You're going to lock up your child's daddy? That won't look good, Emma. It just might put your little clinic out of business."

"Don't bring Sia into this," Emma said. "You may be their father, but you aren't their daddy. How dare you bring Sia into this? How dare you!"

Emma's heart raced as she clenched her hands.

"Look, sweetheart. This can still be a happy reunion for us. I know it's been a while," he said, blowing a kiss in the air. She could practically taste the liquor evaporating from his pores all the way across the room.

"J.D.! We need some back up in here!" Emma called out.

"I just thought you'd be happier to see me is all," Xavier said. "And after all the business I gave you. I bought every last piece of red agate from your pathetic gemstone store. You should be thanking me."

Tap. Tap. Tap.

Emma opened her fists and began tapping the side of her leg, taking a deep breath trying to control her heart rate.

"Deep breaths, deep breaths," she said to herself.

She closed her eyes and focused on how her fingers felt tapping the side of her leg. She felt the air moving in and out of her nostrils as she counted to ten for each inhale and counted to three for each exhale. Her mind raced as she played out a thousand scenarios of what might happen next, from losing custody of Sia to locking Xavier in the county jail. As thoughts ran out of control, Charles' face appeared in her mind. It calmed her, and as she opened her eyes in the bright fluorescent light of the conference room, there he was, standing in the doorway. Charles rushed toward her and wrapped his arms around her waist.

"What the hell?" Xavier shouted out.

Suddenly, Xavier didn't seem so important. In fact, to Emma, he seemed nothing more than mean and pathetic. Emma gathered herself as the fire simmered down from a raging inferno to a cozy burn.

"Look who's here," she said to Charles.

"Pleased to meet you, Xavier," Charles extended his palm toward him. "Sia is a remarkable person. I'm honored to meet their father."

"I bet you are," he said. Xavier stood, his shoulders slumped down. He moved both arms behind his back, refusing to shake Charles' hand. His eyes darted between Emma, Charles, Darrell, and the door. His expression made Darrell suspicious.

"J.D. will be back soon," Darrell said. "He drove Bell home so he could stay the night in his office with Roscoe."

"Thanks for texting me, Darrell. I was halfway across campus trying to catch up with Emma."

"You obsessed with me, too?" Xavier snarled. "Now I see why you two hit it off so well."

"C'mon, Emma. Darrell can take it from here," Charles said. He ignored Xavier's attempt to upset him.

"It's over, Emma," Xavier squawked. "You need to get over yourself. I thought you'd take the hint by now that I don't want seconds of you."

He shot the words like bullets across the room, but they passed right by her. Xavier poured his angry heart out to Emma, and it evaporated. Not a single hateful splatter landed on her. Instead, she straightened her spine, her back arched like a dancer, as she took five steady steps toward the door. Each step echoed in the room's silence as her hips swayed back and forth. Mid-sashay she tapped her side three times and slowly rotated her torso, her neck stretched even higher in the air as her eyes gazed down at Xavier.

"You'll stop this, Xavier. Leave this place alone. This world is wide enough for us both."

Bark! Bark!!

Emma and Charles followed the sound of Roscoe's voice into J.D.'s office while Darrell stayed in the conference room to watch Xavier sober up. Emma gently ran her hand over Roscoe's forehead as Charles scratched a favorite spot just in front of his tail. The pair sat side-by-side in silence for at least half an hour. Nothing needed to be said.

When J.D. returned to the office, Darrell briefed him on the events of the evening. He explained how he and Emma found Xavier passed out in the old theater building. He was backstage, curled up on an old sleeping bag next to a backpack, an empty bourbon bottle, and a plastic bag filled with red agate. Darrell asked J.D. if he wanted to file a police report for trespassing.

"No need," he said. "But can you gather up all the things he left there?"

"Already done."

J.D. thanked Darrell for his service on a long, holiday night and told him he'd take it from there. For the next hour he sat with Xavier in the conference room, one seat away from the man who taunted Roscoe for a month and traumatized Emma for years. When the two emerged a full hour later, Charles and Emma had dozed off, curled up next to Roscoe. They didn't even see Xavier leave.

J.D. covered the two humans with a blanket, then crouched down toward Roscoe. The dog sensed his person and opened his brown eyes, ears perked upwards with a smile wide as the night's sky. Roscoe's medicine had eased his pain. Knowing his dog was comfortable helped J.D. relax. After giving a few head rubs, he leaned back on the couch in his office and closed his eyes, too.

On the morning of July 5th, the three would recount their adventurous Fourth of July, from the drones that lit up the sky to Roscoe's injury, to the expression on Emma's face when she saw her hair in the mirror the day after sleeping on a dog bed all night. It gave the friends a needed laugh over the coffee and donuts Bell delivered. They talked about everything except for one thing: When Charles asked J.D. what happened when he met with Xavier, he answered *"We worked it out."*

The details of whatever J.D. and Xavier said behind closed doors remained a mystery until the timing was right. While Charles and Bell cleaned up from breakfast, J.D. sat down beside Emma. They were alone in his office.

"I want you to know I'm here for anything you need, Emma."

"J.D., I don't need anything. I'm good."

She fidgeted with her hair braids and straightened her gemstone necklace so that it hung in the center of her chest.

"I know you are, but that man has a lot to overcome. He shared his story with me last night."

Emma looked down as though she wanted to crawl in a shell.

"He didn't talk about you. He told me why he came back. He wants to make amends," J.D. explained.

Emma's lips tightened as she asked, "This is what he calls amends?"

"I made a deal with him, Emma. If he breaks it, we have enough on him that he'd spend the next five years in the county jail."

"I can't tell Sia their father is in jail," she said. Her faced stretched long as the new worry of parental incarceration entered her mind.

"I don't think it will come to that. He knows this second chance is also his last chance. I signed him up for a recovery group at the community center. It's run by good people who help men like Xavier get back on track."

"Do you think that's a good idea, J.D.? Think about what he's done to Roscoe."

"I'm not going to take my eyes off of him, Emma."

"You can't watch Roscoe around the clock."

"I mean I'll watch Xavier. My team will know every step he takes. I'm not taking any chances. You're too important to us. We won't put you at risk. But if you have a problem with this—with any of it—tell me. I'll go to the police this morning and end this."

"You really do try to help everyone, don't you?" she asked.

"If I can," he replied. "But not if that means someone I care about gets hurt."

Emma sighed.

"We've got a classic ethical dilemma," she said. "Do we give him a second chance, or do we protect our people?"

"I think we can do both," said J.D. "But only with your blessing."

"I hate ethical dilemmas!" Emma rolled her eyes. "But if you are sure he won't be creeping around me, who am I to stand in the way of a second chance?"

"You can trust me, Emma."

CHAPTER 11

The Recovery

"We got another set of dog bones," Patty shouted. "And a blanket!"

She tossed more tissue paper into the pile in the corner. Each gift bag arrived stuffed with a different pastel color, and it began to look like Patty and J.D. were building a float for an Easter parade. She archived each gift, giving some more attention than others.

"Oh! This one is cookies!"

Patty took a bite, but quickly spit it out, disgusted by the grainy taste.

Crunch. Crunch. Spit!

"Don't eat those!" Patty exclaimed as she tried to wipe off every crumb. "Those are dog cookies! I thought they were from the Variety Bake Shop, not the pet store!"

Patty wasn't deterred from sorting each delivery, sent by Roscoe's fans, who hailed all the way from Scottsboro to Fort Payne. J.D.'s office filled with treats and toys for the dog who captured the hearts of the community.

For the past week and a half, Roscoe had been on bed rest, unable to go outside for his usual rounds around campus. Each night when he saw the flashing lights of the security car pass J.D.'s office window, Roscoe whimpered—he wanted to chase the car, like he used to do, but his vet insisted he stay locked inside until he healed. Roscoe's rear legs didn't seem to improve as much as the dog's determination to move grew. He limped across the office, staring wide-eyed at J.D., begging to be set free from his stay in office jail. Even more pitiful, his new treatment plan included a large white cone wrapped around his neck to keep him from nibbling at his leg. Patty had snapped a pic and posted it on the community center's Roscoe social media page, and the "get well" gifts flowed in by noon.

"Think he can eat with that cone on, Patty?" J.D. asked.

"Oh, he'll find a way," she said as she dropped a dog cookie in front of his snout. Roscoe immediately licked it up, then rested his chin down on his pillow.

"He looks so depressed," J.D. said.

His eyes were half-open and tired. He hadn't been the same since the injury.

"That dog isn't depressed, J.D., he's just bored. He hasn't left this office in a week! Unlike you, Mr. Work-Around-the-Clock, he likes to get out of here from time to time."

"Poor thing. I think he's embarrassed to be seen like this. Maybe we should take this cone off."

"You do that and it's another week of nibbling. He'll never heal and never get out of this office."

"I guess you're right," said J.D.

"Of course, I'm right," Patty laughed. "But it's going to be okay, J.D. Dogs heal. He's tough. Like someone else I know."

She looked down at J.D.'s right leg, stretched out on the couch.

"Don't you think it's kind of strange how similar you two are, J.D.?"

"Me and Roscoe?"

"Yes, you and Roscoe. You both do rounds out here 24/7. Everyone loves you. And now, he's limping around like someone else in this office was not too long ago."

"Oh, that was nothing, Patty. Bell made me have that surgery, truth be told. I was alright before. I'm alright now."

"Bell made you, huh? Dr. Andrew had nothing to do with that? I'm just glad Bell got you to listen."

"It was an old football injury, and now I'm fine."

"Exactly. And Roscoe will be, too. He just needs to be locked in one spot for a few weeks. It worked for you, didn't it?"

"I guess you're right, Patty."

"I guess I am!"

Knock. Knock.

Roscoe's ears perked up when he detected the sound of a visitor outside the office. A familiar Southern voice sang out the hallway.

"Helllooooo? Y'all at work?"

Knock-knock-knock-knock-knock!

The sound was as persistent as the woman behind the oak door.

"I have gifts! Let me in!" Emma shouted, her arms stacked with a basket and several packages.

Inside the office, she laid all the gifts across Patty's desk and explained that she'd collected items for Roscoe from her customers at the animal clinic.

"It's a Poppy thing," she explained. "Ever since we gave that little dog a home, I hear from a lot of people who want to help an animal in need."

"Well, I'm not sure Roscoe is in need," said J.D., his shoulders tightening with stress.

"Look at that pitiful thing," Emma said. "He can't even walk over to see me!"

"He can," said J.D. "He's just taking a break."

"Don't mind him, Emma. J.D. is in a bit of denial that his dog is hurt," Patty said.

"Enough of that! He's going to be fine," said J.D. His brown eyes narrowed and brow wrinkled. "He just needs a rest."

"He must be so embarrassed with that cone around his neck!" Emma said, laughing. "It's so funny! I've got to take a picture of this."

"See? He's embarrassed!" J.D. said, as he bent over to adjust the metal hooks. "Maybe the cone just needs to be loosened a little."

"Now wait a minute, J.D. Don't you want to see his gifts first?" Patty shook a bag that jingled like a Christmas bell.

"He doesn't need less cone," Emma said. "He needs more shine!"

She reached into the pockets of her preppy floral jumper and pulled out something neither Patty nor J.D. had ever seen before.

"That's really something!" J.D. said.

"Look at all those colors!"

They stepped closer to examine the patent leather dog collar that Emma had crafted for Roscoe.

It was adorned with seven crystals in seven different colors: one for health, one for love, one for patience, and one for happiness. The rest were for decoration. She explained how she'd designed it the morning after his accident. Patty and J.D. were mesmerized by its beauty, as well as the thoughtfulness behind its creation.

"I love it!" J.D. exclaimed. "Especially this."

He rubbed a silver plate at the center of the collar, embedded with a tiny quartz crystal. Above the crystal, Emma had engraved Roscoe's name by hand.

"I've been up for a week perfecting this. It has the healing power of all my best gemstones," she explained. "And we've banished red agate from the collection. That one's canceled after you-know-who."

"Xavier!" Patty said under her breath. "Can you believe J.D. didn't lock him up?"

Emma and J.D. looked at each other knowingly. Only they were aware that Xavier entered the center's recovery program the morning after Roscoe's injury.

"Tell us, J.D. What did he say to convince you he wouldn't cause any more pain around here?" Patty asked.

Silence.

"I would have been getting out the salt pellet gun for that one. At the very least he deserves a blast in the butt!" Patty pushed.

Still…silence.

"Seriously, what did he do for you to forgive and forget like that?"

"I didn't forget," he said. "Or forgive. But he does have a second chance."

"I'm sorry I brought him up," said Patty. "But seriously, why'd you let him go? I have to know."

J.D. walked over to Roscoe and held his hand over the dog's chest, as though he was holding onto his heart. J.D. explained, "We made a deal."

"A deal!? I would have beat his butt," Patty laughed. "He better not come back around here."

"Well, that's the thing…he might," said J.D.

"He might?" Patty asked.

Emma looked down, twirling the drawstring on her jumper as though that distraction could keep her heart from racing.

"I asked him to volunteer out here, to help out with the grounds and keep the flowers looking good around the softball field."

"You did what?!" Patty said. "You have to be kidding?"

"I think he needs good people in his life."

"I think we need bad people out of ours!" Patty exclaimed. "And what about Roscoe?"

"I'll take care of Roscoe," said J.D. "I'll keep him safe at all costs."

"What about Emma?" Patty countered.

"We made a deal, too," Emma said. "J.D. and I."

Emma's eyes pooled with reluctant tears as the room closed in around her. Waves of fear, vulnerability, anger, shame, and sadness rose like the water in a hot bath that ran too long. At that moment each emotion competed to be the loudest in her mind. Her tub was about to spill out over the edges. Instead of releasing that energy in front of people, she self-soothed.

Tap. Tap. Tap.

Her index finger bounced on her hip as she slowly breathed in and out.

Tap. Tap. Tap.

She focused on her feet, firmly placed on the ground, telling herself " *You're here. You're standing. You're YOU.* "

Tap. Tap. Tap.

Slowly, a warmth expanded from her belly outward as fear melted away like ice on a brick patio in the summer sun. Her bathtub began to drain.

Tap. Tap. Tap.

She switched fingers, from her index to her middle one, pounding against her leg as if it was Morse code telling her brain she declared independence from the past and no one can change that.

Tap. Tap. Tap.

She watched J.D. and Patty debate whether they'll allow Xavier to volunteer. She chose not to listen. Emma crouched down near Roscoe and rubbed her hand across his dark black coat. On the floor beside him, she fastened the gemstone collar around his neck. The colorful crystals reflected light up and into the cone cinched around his neck. As Roscoe gazed up at her, his big brown eyes seemed even wider with the colors dancing around him in a psychedelic shimmer.

"Are you okay with this, boy?" Emma whispered to him.

He turned his head to the side, like he was thinking. She wasn't asking him about the collar.

"I'm still trying to figure it all out," she said. "That man hurt me, too."

Roscoe licked her arm, his tongue lapping out from the gray around his mouth. In return, Emma tap-tap-tapped her index finger on his temple.

"We're going to be okay, Roscoe," she whispered in his floppy ear. "Sometimes it feels like the past comes back and puts a choke hold on you. But let me tell you a secret about the past: We can let go of it."

Her finger tapping extended into a deep hug as her body unfolded and stretched longways around the dog. She covered Roscoe as he laid his head on her elbow and closed his eyes. They leaned on one another while J.D. and Patty debated. Emma happily tuned out the discussion for as long as she could.

"Emma, it's gorgeous!" Patty exclaimed.

"Huh?" Emma replied. She'd been in a Roscoe daze. She sat up gracefully, her legs crossed over one another and her back stretched out perfectly poised.

"I was so riled up I didn't notice you put that collar on Roscoe!" Patty said. "He looks so dapper."

"He does look dapper, doesn't he?"

"So, Emma, I need to know something," Patty pushed.

Emma took a deep breath, unsure what was coming.

"If Xavier comes back to volunteer, I want to know how you feel about it," Patty paused. "Will you be okay with him around here?"

She slowly rolled her shoulders back, then stood and smoothed out the wrinkles in her cotton jumper. With her feet firmly planted back on the ground, hands on her hips like a superhero, Emma answered.

"I have to be."

"You don't have to," Patty said. "We can ban him from campus. Heck, we can ban him from Jackson County."

"Don't do that. Not for me. In this life we have two choices: give up or keep going. They both hurt. I can't control that man, or any person for that matter. But I can control my heart, my emotions, and if he comes around here...I'll choose to be okay."

"If it ever feels not okay, Emma, tell me. Remember, you have the final say in this," J.D. said. "Your safety is the most important to us."

The rest of the day, the three went through every gift in Roscoe's pile. More blankets. A few chew toys. And even another set of dog cookies, which Patty did her best to convince Emma to taste. Emma wouldn't fall for it.

The outpouring of love motivated J.D. to give back to everyone who supported Roscoe's recovery. Over the next few days, he used extra time at the office spent keeping Roscoe company to develop his plan to construct the statue of the black Lab and Trooper the mustang. It would capture the moment when two wild, animal forces found a connection despite their differences. He quickly put a team together to expedite the project. Barbara agreed to sculpt a 3D version of her original sketch of Roscoe and Trooper touching noses. Darrell measured the grounds at the center of campus, and J.D. choose the spot for the artwork. Patty rallied visitors to the community center to buy more snacks. Every bag of Cheetos, Doritos, and Lay's potato chips purchased in the vending machines increased the funding. Quarter by quarter, J.D. raised enough money not only for the life-size bronze statue to be molded, delivered, and unveiled in the center of campus, but they would also have enough funds for a grand dedication ceremony. People were excited about the project, but they were also worried about the old black Lab. They hadn't seen him in weeks and wondered if he would make it to see his own statue installed on campus.

Roscoe spent all his time in the office and J.D. rarely left his sight. Bell and J.D. considered moving Roscoe home with them, but they worried the Lab wouldn't get along with their twin Golden Retrievers, their giant Sheepadoodle, their squawking bird, and Tobias, son of the famous Poppy. All those animals would be too much for Roscoe's recovery. After all, it only took a toy stuffed dog to send him into a barking fit. Real canine competition could be dangerous.

Even on bed rest, he didn't heal as quickly as anyone wanted. After two weeks in isolation, he still struggled to walk. After three, Roscoe willed himself around with a limp and a smile, but obviously it still hurt to move. J.D. couldn't keep his dog cooped up forever. By mid-August, those sad brown dog eyes begged to go outside so many times that J.D. couldn't resist. He re-opened the doggy door and released Roscoe back out on campus, limp, and all. Maybe the exercise would help him heal, although he feared that at this age, life may be as good as it gets for the Lab.

He was too old for surgery, but young enough in spirit to hold onto his old habits. As the late summer sun blared down on North Star Community Center, Roscoe returned to his rounds. Every day, his slobbery smile beamed as the line cook in the cafeteria slipped him a piece of ham left over from breakfast, and the language teacher tossed him a treat as he trotted past the window to her classroom. In the center of campus, visitors eating lunch on the grassy open space broke off pieces of their sandwiches for him. He did not know the concrete poured in a perfect circle near their eating spot was the foundation for a statue in his honor. Roscoe just kept trotting along his usual route, limping as he roamed.

When he got to the softball field, he got a few head rubs from Xavier, the new volunteer on the grounds team. J.D. had assigned him "Weed and Trash" duty. It was his job to clean up the mess left behind after a game. He'd showed up on time for every shift and group check in for the past month. He kept to himself mostly, other than talking to Roscoe. Xavier noticed the looks he got around campus—what he called "the stank eye" and the sneaky cell phone photos people snapped of him at work. Others wondered what sort of deal he made with J.D. to avoid being kicked out for good. No one except for Emma knew what the two of them talked about that night in his office, yet everyone knew who Xavier was and blamed him for Roscoe's injuries. Everyone except for Roscoe, who sat at Xavier's feet while he tied the strings on a bag full of pulled weeds and garbage from the concession stand.

"Are you okay with this, boy?" Xavier whispered to him. "Being seen with an outcast like me?"

Roscoe turned his head to the side, almost as though he was thinking.

"I'm still trying to figure it all out," he said. "What am I doing here? I'm not wanted."

Xavier reached into his pocket, and Roscoe instinctively licked his arm in anticipation. Instead of a treat, Xavier pulled out a metal medallion depicting a river flowing between three mountains. In the center was the number five, representing five years of sobriety.

"I blew this the moment I got here," he said. "I can't believe all the trouble I caused after I started drinking again."

He stared at the five-year medallion as he flipped it around and around with his fingertips.

"I thought this coin made me immune to it. I came back here after my father died with a stupid plan that maybe I could get some of my life back. Maybe I'd get to meet my child. But you can't come home again when you're a guy like me, Roscoe."

Xavier began to dig a small hole in the soil with his fingers as he talked.

"I got so jealous when I saw all that Emma had built without me. That was always my problem, even seventeen years ago. I loved her, but I never felt good enough for her. She's capable of accomplishing anything she wants, and I'm as worthless as my dad always said I was. When I left our baby, I was doing Emma a favor. It was only a matter of time before she saw that, too."

He placed the sobriety medallion in the hole he'd dug and covered it with soil, careful to smooth over the ground as he buried it.

"Goodbye, five years. Hello, thirty days. My group leader told me recovery isn't a straight line and to value the new start," he said as he took a swig of water from a thermos.

"At least you seem to want me here," he said as he pulled out a chew stick from his pocket. He'd fallen into the habit of keeping them in his work pants for Roscoe. The dog bit into the chew stick as Xavier sat next to him, petting his back.

"When I saw you laying there the night you got hurt, something clicked. It changed me. I never grew up with animals. My dad said they were for hunting, not for hanging around in the house with people. But the way you looked up from that office floor...it was like I could see into your soul. It made me feel horrified at the things I've done to you. And for what? To take out some aggression? I'm pathetic."

The dog kept chewing. Xavier stared at the long row of weeds he needed to pull up by sundown. He knew he needed to get back to work to finish on time. Before he did, he had one last thing to say to Roscoe.

"I'm sorry I hurt you. That will never happen again. You make me feel like everything is going to be okay, Roscoe," he spoke softly near his floppy ear. "Like maybe my past will one day let go of me."

CHAPTER 12

The Cemetery Stroll

Arley sat on the floor in the corner of the den, the short green carpet rubbing against her leg just like it did when she was a child when playing spaceship commander. Now a young woman, she laid on her side, staring face-to-face with her parents' pet rabbit.

"Are you happy here?"

The rabbit's eyes didn't flinch, nor did its oversized floppy feet. The pink toe pads looked so cute to Arley. This bunny could be a poster child for Cadbury. Her mother adopted it without telling her and, as much as having an animal in the house soothed Arley, she felt a bit replaced by it. The sun rose and set to this rabbit's schedule. Every morning at 7 a.m. her mother cleaned its water bottle, freshened the cedar chips in the bottom of its cage, fed it carrots and then—this is the part that just didn't add up to Arley—her mother held it for at least an hour. Every day.

"They'd never leave *you* stranded at the airport," Arley said. "You've really made it around here. You're some-bunny special."

It twitched its nose and moved three hops closer to Arley. Just close enough so Arley could reach out and rub the fur between its eyes.

"You are very cute," she said as she scooped it up and moved to the satin couch. It's feather-stuffed cushions molded around her. "I see why she loves you."

Arley felt at peace with the warmth of the rabbit against her. Its heartbeat calmed her as she brushed its soft fur. As is often the case with animals and people, it became impossible to detect which one relaxed the other first. In the distance, Arley heard the pat of feet on the carpeted steps leading into the foyer. It could only be her mother or her father. As the footsteps moved to the black and white tile Arley could tell by the echoing clicks of stilettos that her mother was coming her way.

"Oh, you two seem to have hit it off!"

Arley forced a smile.

"Isn't she the sweetest? I love that little pink nose," her mother doted. "Let me get you some carrots to feed her."

Click. Click. Click.

Her mother's shoes echoed from the kitchen as she called out instructions in a stream of consciousness cadence.

"So your father and I need you at Cedar Hill Cemetery this afternoon no later than 2 o'clock. I already dropped him off there for the setup while you slept in this morning. You can borrow his car to get there. Unless you want to leave with me now...but you don't look dressed for this. It's a big day for our family, and you should look nice."

"Who died?" Arley asked sarcastically, rolling her eyes from the den.

"Died! No one, God willing. Well, I suppose many people died, actually. It is a cemetery after all. But no one died recently. At least not that I know of."

Click. Click. Click.

"It's the annual Cemetery Stroll, and they are featuring your grandmother today. Aunt Lulu is telling her story."

"Wait, what?" Arley said. "This is the thing where people dress up like their dead relatives and pretend they're back for a day?"

"I wouldn't put it like that."

"The thing where you walk from grave to grave and hear the life story of the person buried there?"

"Arley, the Cemetery Stroll is a day to honor our ancestors by passing on the lessons they taught us, as explained through biographies delivered by their own descendants. It's important! You *must* be there."

"I wish you'd given me a little more notice."

"Everyone knows about the Cemetery Stroll. I'm surprised you didn't already plan to attend," she said as she handed Arley a carrot to feed the bunny. "I'll meet you there at 2 p.m. Your Aunt Lulu will feel hurt if you miss it. She's put a lot of preparation into telling your grandmother's story. The least you can do is listen."

"I get it. I'll be there, mom."

"Thank you, Arley," she said, taking a quick look at the reflection of her auburn hair in the mirror.

Click. Click. Click. Click.

On her way to the front door, her mother turned back toward her daughter and the rabbit.

"And one more thing, you won't leave the rabbit out loose in the house when you come to the cemetery will you? Bunny needs to be caged when we're gone, otherwise she gets into all sorts of messes."

"No, ma'am."

"Don't forget! And be on time! You'll embarrass yourself by showing up late in front of all those people."

Arley's translation: *"Don't embarrass me."*

With the heavy thud of the front door latch slam shut, Arley found herself home alone with Bunny again. She felt its body jolt as the door closed. As its heart raced, it softly nestled into her lap. She stroked its back, gently tapping its temples.

"I know how you feel," Arley said. "She'd love to keep us both in a cage."

The bunny gazed up at her and, in that moment, something snapped. Arley's heart ached from feeling so out of place. She didn't even feel at comfortable in her own body, much less this house. Being here, in her childhood home with all of its expectations and criticisms made her feel less...her. Arley couldn't take it anymore.

"Sometimes it just hurts to exist," she said to herself.

Arley stayed on the couch in the den with the bunny in her lap until the morning sunlight danced through the leaves of the giant magnolia tree. The bunny nibbled the carrot until nothing remained but a tuft of green stalk. Then it hopped down to the carpet and sniffed around. Arley recognized this look.

"Oh, let me get you to your cage, Bunny. Mom will be so mad if you go on the rug!"

But just before she scooped up the animal, Arley thought about what she'd just said. Her mom would be furious if she came home to a pile of rabbit pellets on the floor, especially after insisting Arley keep the pet caged. The only thing that could make her more upset would be if the bunny roamed freely around the house while the family was at the Cemetery Stroll. For Arley, the choice was clear: disobey her mother.

Arley filled the rabbit's bowls with food, more than it could need. She also left out a bunch of carrots, and the rabbit immediately started to binge. Arley could feel revenge coming with every bite. She checked herself in the mirror, lining her smile with fire engine red lipstick. Her mother had ordered her to "look nice." Arley walked out the front door with a smirk on her face; she knew the uncaged bunny would hop around with a belly filled with fiber and leave messy mementos all over the carpet.

She could hardly wait to get to the Cemetery Stroll. The faster it started, the faster she could get home to see her mother's reaction when she discovered Bunny running wild with a trail of rabbit droppings all over the home. Arley planned to play innocent and blame the escape on a faulty cage latch. After all, over the years her mother blamed her for far worse things that she'd never actually done wrong. *"It's karma,"* she thought. Arley's anticipation stayed with her along the windy drive down the mountain, across the B. B. Comer Bridge, and all along Willow Street until she arrived at Cedar Hill Cemetery.

A line of cars already filled the usually empty roadways between the lawns of burial plots on the other side of the iron gates. The Cemetery Stroll brought more than a hundred people to the grounds and, because of all the attention today, family plots were decorated with large flower arrangements and fresh landscaping. Among it all, Arley watched the costumed performers gather on the hill near the oldest graves in town. The tombstones looked different in this older section, with some carved into towering angels. Others were concrete tree stumps to honor former members of the Woodmen of the World. The ancestors dressed as though they were from another time. Arley saw a woman in a long white gown twirling a parasol. Another presenter was dressed as a farmer, while yet another wore a judge's robe. The featured families prepared to share their relatives' life story in the words and style of their own ancestor. On the horizon, away from the older section of graves, Arley noticed her friend, Emma, placing flowers on a headstone far from the ceremony.

"Emma!"

She was too far away to hear her, and Emma's focus was on a small, rectangular grave marker anyway. Arley moved against the stream of arrivals until she was within a few feet of Emma.

"Hey you!"

"Arley! Oh, you startled me."

Emma wore summer sandals and a colorful shell draped over her body. Her outfit appeared more beach-ready than gravesite couture. Her face, however, looked like she'd been crying.

"I'm not really here for the stroll. I'm just visiting. I've felt a little lonely lately. Sia is still away at her summer job, and I guess you could say I missed my family."

Arley looked down at the tombstone engraved simply "Frances" and realized the grave belonged to Emma's mother.

"Oh," Arley awkwardly stumbled backwards as she muttered "I didn't realize. I'm sorry to disturb you."

"Child, you can't wake the dead! You aren't disturbing nobody. Besides, my mama would like you. A lot. You've got sass like me. I wish I could introduce you to her. So much has changed since we lost my mama. I hope she's able to sense some of it. There's so much I'd like to tell her."

"Are you going to tell Frances' story today?"

"Me? Oh, I'd like that very much. Not a day goes by where I don't think of her. I believe the prayers she spoke still cover me now."

"What would you say if you were sharing her story today?"

"Oh, that's a good question, Arley. She was everything to my family. It's hard to tell stories about people like that and do them justice," Emma said. "But I'd probably share how my mama almost moved away from around here. She would have been my age then. My daddy got a job in Tampa, and I think that may have been her happiest and saddest time all at once, though she never said that."

"Happiest and saddest?"

"Oh, happy and sad can live together. Especially when you're pulled away from a place that holds your heart. And she was. Mama got pulled away from Tampa, and the beautiful house my daddy bought for her there on Bayshore Boulevard. They never got to move in."

"What happened?"

"Well, sometimes tragedy strikes out of the blue. Her brother-in-law died in a terrible accident. Then her father died of a heart attack not long after—such a sad year for her with so much loss. The family needed my mama, so she moved back here with my daddy...and things really changed."

"What happened?"

"Well...I was born! I like to think I was the rainbow after the rain. After those funerals and all that grief, it wasn't my mama and daddy's time to stay in Florida. So, they stayed here. Home. I like to think I inherited my mama's sense of adventure and bravery though...her drive to try new things."

"Life can really turn on a dime, huh?"

"Oh, it does, honey. It does. And it will for you one day, too. Good and bad. It always happens."

Arley's eyes widened with both fear and excitement about the prospect of change. She peered up the hill and saw her mother standing by Aunt Lulu, dressed in her grandmother's old blue silk housecoat. It looked oddly informal among the people in costumes that dated back through the decades. Lulu wore the vintage 1960s robe so well. She could turn an old button down into a fashion statement. Arley wished her mother was more like her Aunt Lulu. She wondered how two sisters could be so different. Arley never knew the woman who raised them. Her grandmother died a few months before Arley was born. It always felt like ancient history, but Arley realized her grandmother's death must have affected her own family story. She wished she had been the rainbow after the rain for her own mom. How painful it must have been to lose her mother just before giving birth to her. It almost made Arley feel badly that she let the bunny loose in the house. Almost.

At precisely 2 p.m. the presentations began as scheduled. A small audience gathered at each grave to hear soliloquies from their neighbors, who shared their ancestor's legacy on repeat. The past came to life as Cyndi reenacted her grandmother Octavia's life story, describing how she finished college in an era when many women couldn't go, yet she eventually became a teacher herself. David explained how his great-grandfather Turner moved the family to Alabama and fought for the Union Army in the Civil War when it was dangerous to be anything but a Confederate in the South. Each presenter shared stories for ten minutes or less, then the cluster of a crowd moved on to the next grave to hear the next life story. All but one. Arley's mom never moved. She stayed to watch Lulu channel their mother again and again and again like the past got stuck on repeat. Arley's father stood behind his wife, gently touching the arch of her back in comfort, as she watched the presentation six times in a row. Arley, on the other hand, made rounds to every grave except her own grandmother's. She knew she had to face the past but wasn't ready to hear it until the very last set of presentations.

Arley watched as Aunt Lulu got into character one last time. She looked down at the ground as her blue silk robe blew around her ankles in the breeze. Arley noticed her mother was staring intensely, her hand clutched over her chest, as if her own mother may return any moment for one last visit. Lulu took a deep breath and dramatically jolted her head up, eyes wide open and her arms tossed up in the sky.

"Sometimes," Lulu shouted, channeling Arley's grandmother "it hurts to exist."

The line hit so close that it took Arley's breath away. Immediately, she felt cosmically connected to her grandmother. The crowd awkwardly chuckled at this bold beginning of the family story. Lulu shared every twist and turn, from triumph to tragedy. Whenever life got pretty good for her grandmother, the universe seemed to tell her "Uh-uh, not yet." She was first in her family accepted to college but, when she arrived, the school had no record of her dorm reservation. She slept in the library her first month. Her life brought love and loss, and it was often painful. Her first serious boyfriend slipped off a waterfall in Cheaha State Park when he was pulling out a ring to propose to her. They never got married, because he fell for his emergency room nurse and married her just six weeks later. Her only trip overseas resulted in a case of measles. And when she finally got her first home, a tornado blew the roof two streets over before she could finish unpacking. Yet every time things seemed insurmountable, some amazing pivot always seemed to happen to her grandmother. For example, her next house had a basement. Her next boyfriend chased her more than he chased waterfalls. And when she was sleeping in that library, she completed an entire semester of reading in just one month. When life gave her lemons, she made a lemon margarita.

Lulu's talent as a natural entertainer shined. Years of vying for her mother's attention as a child taught her more than any theater camp could have. The crowd ate up her graveside presentation, but Arley couldn't help noticing there was very little mention of her grandmother's children. Not Lulu. Not her mom, either. Her grandfather barely got a mention besides the story about how he almost burned the house down while frying turkey one Thanksgiving. That tale ended with pie for dinner.

Arley found the lack of connections strange, as most of the Cemetery Stroll tales focused on family. Arley got the impression that her grandmother wasn't around too often for her children and, when she was, she was more concerned with her own needs than theirs. It always seemed to be about her, which was also what made her grandmother's story so fun to hear. But a good story does not make a good mom. Arley wondered if, these days, her grandmother would have been called a narcissist, only seeking satisfaction for her own wants and unafraid to inhale all the emotional energy in the room. Maybe having a narcissist as a mother was a trait Arley shared with her own mom, she wondered.

Clap. Clap. Clap.

In a blink, the allotted ten minutes passed, and the presentation ended similarly to how it began.

"Sometimes, it may hurt to exist," Lulu said as an encore, her tone soft and wise this time, "But life is meant to be lived through the pain, not inside of it."

As the crowd clapped again, Arley felt something swell inside that she hadn't experienced all summer. A warm desire bubbled up to go hug her mother. So, she did. And her mother hugged her back. Hard. Arley felt a tear drop on her arm, unable to discern if it was hers or her mother's.

"Thank you for making me come here today, mom."

"Oh, Arley, I guess I forced this on you, huh? I'm so sorry."

"It's okay. I didn't know all those stories about grandma. I'm glad I came."

Her mother reached toward her, as though she was going to adjust her hair as usual, but she stopped herself. Instead, her she adjusted her own hair and looked into her daughter's eyes.

"Arley, I think I've been treating you an awful lot like how my mother treated me, and I don't want that. I don't want you to ever feel captive by me. I want you to—" she paused as tears welled in her eyes. "I want you to dance!"

"Dance?" Arley seemed confused.

The nineteen-year-old became so accustomed to taking orders from her mom, she began thinking of what dance move she'd perform in the middle of Cedar Hill Cemetery to obey her request. Arley stretched out her arm, bent her knee and began swaying her head back around in a figure eight motion like there was music playing.

"Arley!" Her mother said, exploding in laughter. "That's not what I meant—"

Her mother stopped herself. Instead of correcting her daughter, she danced, too. Aunt Lulu's mouth dropped as she snapped a picture of Arley and her sister dancing by their mother's grave. Her shock turned into hysterical laughter, as the stress they'd all been under from the Cemetery Stroll evaporated among the dogwood trees. Sometimes digging into the past brings out the weird in everyone.

"This isn't what I meant exactly by dancing," her mother said, as the two of them leaned and swayed to an imaginary beat. "I was speaking in a metaphor!"

"Well, it's too late now I think," Arley replied, the laughter taking over. "We are doing this!"

Her mother giggled, something Arley hadn't seen her do in years.

"When I said I want you to dance, I just meant I want you to live. I want you to be free. I want you to do whatever you want whether I like it or not!"

"Like dancing at the cemetery!" Lulu shouted out, joining the silent goth dance party.

"What have you done with my mom?" Arley said, as the three collapsed in laughter onto the concrete bench by the headstone.

"I think the visit from our mama at the Cemetery Stroll may have brought out some old memories," Lulu said. "And some of them weren't happy ones."

"I was just telling your niece," Arley's mom explained, "That she has permission to listen less to her mother and more to her own voice."

"You don't have to listen to everybody," Lulu said, "But you've got to listen to yourself!"

"She's right," her mother added. "And I need to learn to let go. I tried to, Arley. I tried all summer to stay out of your way, to give you space to be you. Then I'd panic, and I'd worry I'm screwing it all up."

"I'm getting mixed messages here," Arley said. "You're saying the reason you haven't been around is so I can be...me?"

"Yes, sort of," her mother said. "I don't know. I feel like I've screwed up. My mother was rarely around, and when she was, then it was like we were her property. Like we were born to serve her."

Arley watched her curiously, as though she was seeing her as a person, not just a mother, for the first time. Her mother spoke about her grandmother in a way Arley recognized because it's how she often spoke about her own mother. She wasn't sure how to process this revelation, but it seemed big. It felt real. It appeared that her mother was trying. Maybe her hot-then-cold behavior this summer was more about her own issues than her disapproval of Arley.

"I wanted you to be the best version of yourself. But now I see that what I considered guidance may have come across as criticism."

"It's okay, mom. I think I get it."

"The worst thing is, I'm afraid I was holding you back. The best version of yourself is yourself!"

"Thank you for saying that mom. But, you know, there are some things I'm going to need your opinion on."

"And I'll give it. But only when you ask," her mother said. "Arley, I am in awe of you. Not only do you make me proud, but you've moved so far beyond me at your age. I can't wait to see what you do next."

"I think you two need a do-over," Lulu said. "Why don't you do a summer reset?"

"A reset?" Arley asked.

"A do-over," Lulu shrugged.

"I have an idea," her mother said. "For what's left of the summer, when you want me around or you want my opinion on something, just tell me. I'll be there. And when you want to do something without me around, just do it. I promise not to pester you."

"Sounds like a deal to me!"

While the crowd dwindled down around them, Arley's dad walked up toward the three women. With his volunteer assignments complete, he was ready to catch up.

"What did I miss?" he asked.

They shared more stories about Arley's grandmother, including a few from her dad. He remembered how she'd never once allowed her children to own a pet.

"I knew your mom was missing you terribly last fall, Arley, when she adopted Bunny," her dad explained.

"I never had a pet before then! Your grandmom always called them too messy," her mother frowned.

She confessed it required great courage on her part to adopt the rabbit, despite all her lifelong warnings about the sanitary dangers of keeping an animal in the house. It had been one of her best decisions, although she still struggled with the cleanliness.

"The rabbit!" Arley thought, remembering how she'd freed it to wreak havoc while they were away. She made up an excuse to skip dinner with her parents and instead rushed home to scrub, disinfect, and deep clean every fiber of the house in a desperate attempt to undo the disaster she'd left waiting for her mother. Her act of rabbit-defecating defiance suddenly felt more like an attack on the progress the two had made at the cemetery.

With each rabbit pellet she discovered in the carpet, she regretted her inner child outburst, but she cleaned everything to perfection. Moments before her mother and father walked in the door to their home, Arley plopped herself back on the green satin couch in the den, with the house immaculately scrubbed all around her. With the bunny sitting in her lap, just as it had in the morning, Arley felt proud of her day spent cleaning up the mess. And not just the one left by the rabbit.

CHAPTER 13

Unveiled

"Welcome to Roscoe's lounge!"

At the entrance, Chasley greeted the line of co-workers and friends one by one, as if ushering passengers onto an airplane.

"Welcome! Please step over to the refreshment area."

She pulled back a silver-beaded curtain revealing the event space, which usually served as a small study room in the administration building. She and Julise had transformed the typical beige-on-beige aesthetic into a sparkle fest, with silver and gold decorations that flowed across every inch from floor to ceiling. If they could wrap foil around something, they did.

"Drinks are self-service. Please enjoy!"

In the center of the wall, a small spotlight illuminated the framed photo of the famous black Labrador Retriever. The bronze statue in his likeness was to be unveiled in just a few hours. Chasley had driven Roscoe to Cutie Patootie's in Scottsboro to have his pet portrait taken just for this occasion. J.D. requested "nothing too cute" and the doggy photographer agreed to take a scholarly shot worthy of a distinguished dog, despite an array of costumes available for the photo shoot. If she'd photographed him in the hot dog suit or wearing the sunflower cap, she would have never heard the end of it. Above the beautifully lit photograph, Chasley hung a custom banner with the words "Roscoe Unveiled!" printed across it. Each letter hung down on a tiny triangle tab connected to a golden braid. Plates of finger foods labeled "Statue Sliders," "Trooper's Trail Mix," and "Dedication Day Desserts" were spread around a giant glass bowl filled to the brim with "Roscoe's Punch." Chasley and Julise had outdone themselves with yet another community center renovation: they turned the drab study area into a reception hall worthy of celebrating an important new artwork.

"Eat and drink, everybody!" Chasley called out. "This is for you! And especially you, Roscoe!"

The old black Lab wagged his tail in the center of the room, surrounded by his fans. The VIP reception was originally planned for the "J.D.C. Day" crowd that gathered on Wednesdays, but a few other special guests heard about the party and slipped their names onto the list. They all arrived ahead of the Roscoe Statue dedication, gathering to snack and socialize before the unveiling. Outside, the life-size bronze statue remained shrouded in secrecy; in fact, it had been hidden during the entire construction phase. Only Barbara, who designed it, and Patty, who couldn't resist peeking behind the heavy tarp covering it, had seen the completed piece of art, which was positioned in the center of campus. J.D. hadn't even seen it—he wanted to be as wowed by the unveiling as the rest of his team.

"Are these for Roscoe or for us?" Patty asked Chasley, pointing to the cookies on the dessert tray. She didn't want to bite into another dog treat by mistake.

"For us! Roscoe's treats are over there," Chasley said, pointing to the "Canine Charcuterie Board," piled high with his favorite meats, sliced cheeses, and beef jerky. Amy placed it on a special platter so Roscoe wouldn't have to strain his sore neck to eat. But greeting his guests took precedence over noticing his food, which was highly unusual for the dog. He had been eating less and less lately, ever since the accident. Today, even his limp couldn't hold back his slobbery smile and thumping tail as he seemed to dance from person to person around the room.

"Is he going to eat that pepperoni?" Anna asked.

She stood hand in hand with her cousin Lilah, both of their eyes locked on the fancy doggy charcuterie board, which sat about six inches off the floor on a tray labeled "For Roscoe."

"I don't know, Anna. There are plenty of treats for all of us people. But if you want to eat the dog's snacks, you'll have to get down there and eat it like a dog would," Patty said, expecting to detract her granddaughter. Instead, it encouraged her.

"Okay!" Anna blurted out, as she fell to her knees and crawled over to the dish, pretending to be a dog.

"Oh, Anna!" Patty sighed. "You've gone to the dogs!"

"Bark! Bark!" Anna yelped out, as she went into full canine character. She scratched for fleas and wagged her imaginary tail as she pretended to eat the pepperoni and sniff the cheese slices.

"Just ignore her," Patty suggested.

Anna's dog act got louder and more rambunctious, until Lilah joined in the fun. Then it became all-out chaos. The pair chased each other around the reception room, barking and yelping. Anna accidentally caught her arm on a streamer tied to the banner on the wall, which yanked the long cloth down with a powerful force. Anna didn't realize she was dragging the banner behind her even as it whipped around like a pressure washer hose left unattended.

"Stop it, Anna! I'm going to put you in the doghouse!"

That just encouraged Anna to go harder. The banner got tangled on a table leg as Anna leapt up to give puppy kisses to Patty. Suddenly, the banner jolted the table so that every snack plate shook and "Roscoe's Punch" rippled in the glass bowl and splashed out the sides. With all eyes on the table, no one noticed Lilah on the other side of the room. Her puppy act involved rolling around on her back, like a dog in the grass. As she flipped and twisted her body, she ran into her cousin. The banner pulled the table with such force that...BOOM! Every treat from the "Statue Sliders" to the "Dedication Day Desserts" crashed down into a pile on the floor amidst shards of the broken punch bowl.

"Nobody move!" Patty yelled out. "We don't want to step on glass around here."

J.D. crouched down at Roscoe's side to keep him from stepping on any pieces of glass. The old dog looked up at him as if he knew he was being protected.

"I'll call Darrell to help clean this up," Chasley said.

"Actually, he's on statue duty," J.D. exclaimed. "I'll text Xavier. He's volunteering today."

Chasley looked at Julise, who looked at Trish, who looked at Brenda, who looked at Patty, who finally said what they were all thinking: "What the heck is Xavier doing here today? On Roscoe's day?"

"It's all hands on deck," J.D. explained. "We need all the volunteers we can get with so many people coming on campus."

"Look, J.D., I know you are all about second chances, but everybody has been talking about all the trouble he caused out here."

"He's shown up to volunteer for every shift, usually early. The grounds around the softball field have never looked better. He's a hard worker."

"But after what happened at the Latino Festival, and then with Roscoe, everybody says—"

"If I worried about every negative thing anyone said, I'd get nothing done around here."

"I guess that's true," Patty said, thinking of her own longstanding rule of working with J.D.: *Never be negative.* Instead, she said, "If there's a way he can safely help around here, it will be done!"

Ding. Ding. Ding.

"Okay, everyone...let's move this to the theater building. I've been texting my team and they put together some snacks from the cafeteria over there," Chasley said.

"You mean you two planned a back-up reception, just in case?" Patty asked. "We knew y'all are good, but this is next level!"

One by one, every guest, including the canine of honor, carefully stepped out of the wrecked reception room and moved to the theater building. On her way out, Patty saw Xavier coming down the hall with a mop and a trash bag. She nodded her head pleasantly as she passed him, but her eyes conveyed her thoughts: *Don't screw this up.*

For the next half hour, Xavier worked alone, brushing away every trace of a mishap. Finally, as Xavier rehung the banner, he could hear familiar footsteps coming down the hallway. Even after almost twenty years, he sensed when Emma approached him. As he turned around, all the color drained from his face. She was framed in the wooden entrance way with one hand on her hip and one leg stretched long to the side. Her spiral hair bloomed up from her arched eyebrows, and she wore a yellow dress covered in white daisies. She appeared cautious, but confident. He appeared broken, but hopeful.

"Did you shut down the party?" Emma asked.

"They moved it to the theater after—" his throat tightened from nerves. "After an accident."

"Is everybody ok?"

"Yes. No one was hurt, other than the snacks," he held up the trash back. "I cleaned up the mess for J.D."

"Good."

"Did you cause the accident, Xavier?"

"No."

"Good."

"It was one of the kids just having fun," he explained.

"That happens with kids sometimes," she said. "But you wouldn't know about kids, would you?"

He looked down.

"You know they're going to be here, today."

"Who?"

"Sia."

"Our baby?"

"My child," she said sternly.

"Does she know I'm here?"

"It's they, not she. Sia knows your story, even though they just got back from summer camp last week. Everyone knows some man stalked a poor beloved dog and caused who-knows-what-else kinds of trouble," Emma paused to breathe and said the next part slowly, with intention. "But no one, and I mean no one, knows that man is Sia's father—except for my very close friends."

"Are you going to tell her I'm her father?"

"It's they."

"I'm sorry. I'm still getting used to pronouns," he said.

"Mmm-hmm," she crossed her arms. "Catch up."

"Are you going to introduce Sia to—" he stopped a moment to get the pronoun right, "To their father?"

"Sia is *my* child," she paused. "Even if they are almost eighteen. I won't force an introduction. Sia will choose...but not today."

"I understand. Thank you, Emma."

She stared at the man who once held so much power over every part of her life. Seventeen years ago, she believed he was the sun and she was the moon, basking in his light. She thought she could only glow by reflecting what he offered the world. That just wasn't true, she realized. Not then. Not now. All this time nothing revolved around him. Not her business. Not her success. Not her failure. Certainly not the child she had with him. He didn't illuminate any of it. Crying over him was crying over nothing. He was not the sun—she was. And is. At this moment, she saw him lost in darkness.

"Why are you here, Xavier?"

"Because J.D. asked me to clean up the mess."

"No, why are you back here? You abandoned us. And now you're back, chasing some dog around town and throwing rocks at it? It doesn't get much lower than that. Tell me why you are here."

"When I said clean up the mess, I didn't mean *this* mess," He pointed to the wrecked reception snacks. "J.D. asked me to clean up *my* mess. We made a deal the night Roscoe got hit by the car. He said if I made things right with you, he wouldn't turn me in for trespassing, for the bad things I did around here...not for any of it."

"Mmm-hmm," she said. "So, what's your plan? How are you going to fix this...mess?"

"I don't know. But showing up here at the community center is my start."

"Why did you even come back here in the first place? It's been seventeen years."

"After I left town," his eyes stared at the ground. "After I left you and Sia, everything fell apart. I knew I had ruined everything."

"You ruined nothing," she fired back. "Sia is wonderful. And I am, too...now."

"You always were wonderful. I was not," he explained. "After I left, the work dried up. My confidence dried up. I just drove. I didn't know where I'd end up, and I didn't really care. I wanted to be a thousand miles from myself."

"Where did you go?"

"I went to hell when I left you, and I never came back. I was a nomad, wandering all over. And this is all I have to show for it."

His keyring jangled as he held up his collection of old keys from all the short-term rentals and sublets that didn't work out for him.

"I couldn't keep a job. I started drinking to pass the time, and I couldn't stop. Things got so bad I ended up in jail one night in Knoxville. That's when I swore off alcohol and got some help. I stayed sober for five years. But I lost that, too, when I came back here."

"Why did you come back, Xavier?"

"I...wanted to say I'm sorry."

"By throwing *my* red agate at a *dog*?"

Her Southern accent stretched out the word dog, stressing both her charm and the burning fire inside her at the thought of where Xavier had been all those years.

"I'm sorry for that, too. I see Roscoe so differently now. I was a fool. When I came down and heard about you and your clinic with Charles—all that success—I lost myself, and I lost control. I heard that story everyone tells about how you all rescued that dog from the side of Langston Road...something just came over me. I went to the clinic to get a peek at your life, but then I got angry."

"Mm-hmmm. So, was that your narcissism or toxic masculinity taking over? By the way, I don't accept either of those anymore. You were angry? At me? You left, Xavier. Were you angry I didn't chase after you? Angry I didn't beg you back? Angry that I survived you?"

His shoulders slumped down, his white t-shirt hung off him as if it was one size too large. He rubbed his hand down the side of his scraggly beard, pulled off his cap and looked up at Emma as helpless as a little boy.

"It was jealousy. You have everything. I have nothing. But I wasn't angry at you. I was angry at myself for all of it. For leaving seventeen years ago. For hurting Roscoe. For everything I've done to hurt you. I was angry I turned out just like my father said I would—worthless. He went to the grave reminding me of that. And he's right."

Emma stared at the man who'd caused so much trauma in her life, a burned-out sun whose bitterness pulled so strongly that his own gravity had crushed him. All this time her perception was wrong. Looking up at his six-foot frame, she somehow felt taller than Xavier. Not because of what he lacked in his life, or because he admitted his mistakes. That felt satisfying to hear, but it wasn't as important to her as she had imagined, nor was it the source of her confidence. That came from the life she'd built on her own. She didn't need Xavier or his apology. As the realization hit, Emma slapped her knee, through her daisy-coated yellow dress.

"Damn it!" Emma exclaimed.

"I didn't mean to upset you," Xavier said.

"No, I'm not upset at you. It's just, well...damn it!!"

She punched her fist in the air and squinted her brown eyes as she realized letting go of her resentment toward Xavier actually meant she didn't have to be upset anymore. She didn't have to be anxious anymore. She didn't have to feel anything at all toward him anymore.

"Ugh!" She sighed as her face relaxed. Emma put her palms on her head as a new fundamental truth echoed through her mind. "I think—No, I know that I must forgive you. And maybe one day I can forget."

"Emma, really?"

"One day. Look, Xavier, you didn't ruin my life. You just left it. And I rose above it *on my own*."

"You rose above me on your own, even before I left," he said.

"For this to work, you must respect my boundaries. You can't get jealous of my business or my relationship with Charles. He's a good man, Xavier."

"You deserve that."

"And I want you to hear one thing clearly," she said. "Forgiveness does not require reconnection. Not with me. Not with my child."

"I understand."

"But my child," she paused and corrected herself. "*Our* child is eighteen next month. The choice will be Sia's. Not mine. It's up to them. And it sure won't be a choice made because you sprung it on us."

"Thank you."

"We'll see what happens, Xavier. Today, I choose to rise above the past. Today...I forgive you. Tomorrow depends on you. No more throwing rocks."

With a turn of her shoulders, she walked away from a burden she'd carried for seventeen years. All this time, she thought moving on meant never forgetting the pain he'd caused her. Instead, healing meant letting go of it. As the sound Emma's footsteps faded down the hall, Xavier pulled a 30-day sobriety coin out of his pocket and held on tight.

By mid-afternoon, the reception wrapped, and the crowd moved outside for the statue unveiling. More than two hundred people gathered in the grassy common area at the community center. Familiar faces filled the lawn, including several VIPs who'd attended that fateful presentation when Roscoe crashed J.D.'s pitch. Had J.D.'s speech gone as planned, the statue may have only been a mustang. There were also quite a few people in attendance who'd witnessed the shocking moment at the Latino Festival when the infamous banner dropped on stage. But had that not happened, the horse and black Lab would have never touched noses in that so well-known pose. As J.D. put it *"Something bad happened. Then something wonderful happened."*

The crowd formed a circle around the tarp-covered statue. Emma wrapped one arm around Sia and held Charles' hand with the other. Bell stood just a few feet away, dressed beautifully in a blue wrap the color of her eyes. If either had been any bluer, she may have blended in with the perfect summer sky. Arley waved at them across the lawn, whispering *"Those are my friends"* to her mom from the other side of the circle.

"You can go to them," she said. "I'll be okay here."

Arley felt free for the first time all summer. When the chains of expectations lifted, something unexpected happened; she actually wanted to spend time with her mother.

"Okay, I'll watch with them," Arley said. "But let's ride home together. We'll get dinner."

Arley darted across the circle, crossing paths with the canine guest of honor. The sun beamed down on him like a spotlight. His multi-colored gemstone collar from Emma sparkled on everything he passed, including the faces of the many people who called out his name, hoping he'd accept a treat or a pet on the head. Roscoe clearly recognized this day was for him. Like a skilled politician, he moved from person to person, looking up at each with his big, brown eyes and slobbery pink smile as if saying *"Thank you for coming to support me today!"* His tail wagged non-stop and, as he approached J.D., his entire backside wiggled with so much excitement he appeared to be dancing. In the warm Southern air, Roscoe leaned against J.D.'s leg, looking up as the dog stretched his back leg straight out to the side. The unnatural position was a clear indicator that Roscoe was in pain, despite his joy. All the prancing from guest to guest took a toll on his bad leg, but he persevered. When pain and love live side-by-side, a dog's heart beats stronger than the sting.

"It's time!" J.D. whispered, bending down to eye level with Roscoe. Face to face, human and dog stared at one another with pure adoration. Roscoe wouldn't interrupt J.D.'s presentation this time. The dog stood in the center with him from the start.

"Like so many good things in life, there are many mysteries and wonders that led to this statue being here," said J.D., speaking from a wooden podium just to the side of the tarp-covered statue. "I have some things to say about this statue—probably too much! I told Bell everyone would just have to endure it!"

"Hear that?" Emma whispered. "You got the first shout out, Bell! And it made the crowd laugh, too!"

J.D. retold the tale of how he'd tried to make this statue a reality for years, even traveling to New Mexico in search of an artist to cast a bronze mustang in honor of the community center's mascot.

"Too cost prohibitive," J.D. explained, his disappointment echoing over the loudspeaker. "But that was before Roscoe."

The black Lab looked up at his person, tail wagging, crowd cheering. It was one of those moments when the applause just kept rolling, and Roscoe knew it was for him.

"So how did we pay for it? Well, I made a contract with a vending machine company where the community center got a small percentage of the sales off snacks. I wanted to spend that money on something special since it was your money spent on Cokes, Dr. Peppers, Snickers, and Cheetos from our vending machine: Thank you for that support! And I hope you had a good snack. That's where the money for this work of art came from."

"That's a lot of Cheetos!" Patty yelled out.

"I realize we had some people like Patty encouraging you to make a few extra purchases for the cause," J.D. laughed. "Even today, Heather and Rachel are selling Roscoe t-shirts to fund our scholarship program. But this statue is about so much more than even our beloved Roscoe."

J.D. explained how the statue's designer, Barbara, came up with the idea of building a bronze replica of Roscoe, the campus dog, right beside a statue of Trooper, the real-life mustang.

"These two animals symbolize a place that cares for you like family, no matter where you come from. A place where everyone is free to be the best person you can," J.D. locked eyes with Xavier for what he said next. "And I mean everyone."

Emma spotted Xavier in the crowd and nodded her head.

"Everyone," she whispered to herself, as Charles squeezed her hand.

"We see Roscoe and Trooper as symbols of how to treat people here at North Star. I hope that for decades and decades to come this statue, of this very unlikely pair, will give people peace, amusement, and inspiration. May these bronze characters remind all that no matter our different backgrounds, we can find common ground when we respect each other."

And with that, the unveiling began. J.D. reached up for a rope cable, just like he had at the Latino Festival, as the countdown started.

"10...9...8..."

He wrapped the rope around his hand as Patty and Bell walked over to stand on each side of him.

"7...6...5..."

The crowd's boisterous enthusiasm took over the countdown. It overpowered any sound delivered into the mic and over the loudspeaker.

"You sure this is going to work, J.D.?" Patty said. "I mean the last time you pulled a rope didn't turn out so well."

"4...3...2..."

"Trust him, Patty!" Bell smiled. "He's got this."

"I'm ready, Patty. Let's do it."

"One!"

They pulled the rope and the tarp slowly peeled down the bronze statue. Inch by inch, the work of art was revealed. First, the mustang's wavy metal mane shimmered in the sun, then its strong back and flowing tail emerged from the covering. It was an exact replica, measured and made to stand the same height and build as Trooper. As the tarp fell to the ground, the black Labrador was revealed. The contours of Roscoe's fur rolled like rivers in bronze, adding texture that made the statue appear lifelike. The dog's sculpted eyes gazed up at the horse as the pair touched noses, just as they had done that fateful day at the Latino Festival. Proof that if two wild species can connect, tolerate, and accept their differences, surely two humans could, too.

Bark! Bark! Bark-Bark!

Even Roscoe seemed to cheer.

"He's not very good with other dogs on campus, but he seems fine with this one!" J.D. laughed, as

Roscoe ran up to stand beside his sculpted likeness. "But there's one thing missing...and that's the surprise today."

Gasps could be heard as that surprise made its way through the rear of the crowd. The energy from the cheers transformed into startled amusement. There was movement within the circle as dozens of people stepped aside, parting so the special guest could take his place in the center by the statue.

"It's magical and wonderous!" Arley and Sia said in unison. They were the first to make the connection about what was coming next, but neither expected to hear those exact words from someone else. They each turned to see who could have possibly said such a specific description at the same time they did.

Again, the pair spoke in unison, "You must listen to Bonnie Tyler!"

"I thought I was the only one who knew that old song," Sia said. "My mom played it all the time when I was a kid."

"Same! Well, sort of. Your mom played it all the time while you were at camp this summer!" Arley laughed. "It's so nice to meet you...finally!"

"Same!"

Amidst the celebrations, with the crowd roaring around them, Sia and Arley found the magic and wonder in discovering a kindred spirit.

"Wait," Emma said, as she realized what was coming. "Is that who I think it is?"

Through the rows of people across the lawn, Trooper the mustang emerged. Amber Rain, his trainer, led the real-life horse through the crowd as he pranced straight toward Roscoe and their statue. She smiled with pride as the mustang captivated the audience. Trooper dipped his head down to the dog as Roscoe lifted his neck toward the horse and, just like at the Latino Festival, the unlikely friends touched noses in real life as their immortal bronze counterparts stood in silhouette doing the same.

"What a day!" Patty exclaimed.

"I'll never forget it," said J.D. "I'll never forget this."

J.D. sat on the bench near the statue for hours and watched every visitor snap photos with the statue and the real-life dog. Bell never left his side.

"I'm so proud of you," she said. "You bring out the best in people."

"I think it's that dog that brings out the best in me," he said.

"Hey you two!" Arley called out to them as the campus streetlights clicked on. The quaint, round globes automatically illuminated as daylight ran out of time.

"Arley! Thank you so much for coming," J.D. said.

"Oh, I couldn't miss this! But I have to get going. I have packing to do. I fly back to Texas tomorrow."

"Back to school already?" exclaimed Bell.

"I didn't want to tell you I was leaving just after the statue dedication. I was afraid it would make the celebration feel like a goodbye."

"I understand what it's like to want just one more day."

"The summer goes fast!" J.D. said. "But it always comes back. And I hope you will, too."

"I wanted to thank you both. This summer meant a lot to me."

Arley felt Roscoe at her hand and smiled as his warm lick coated her knuckles.

"I feel like everything sort of changed for me this summer," she said. "I feel so much more...me. And it feels good! It's thanks to all our adventures out here together."

"We had a few, didn't we?" J.D. said. "We will miss you."

"And I'll miss you! Almost as much as him!"

She kneeled and gave Roscoe a big hug around his neck, squeezing him so tightly, like she'd never see her dog friend again.

"Take good care of J.D. and Bell, ok ol' boy?"

"Remember Arley," J.D. advised, "you can always come home. Don't let anyone tell you any different. But when you're away...be away! Soak it all up. It'll give us something new to talk about when you come back to visit!"

Arley left with her mom for their dinner date, but not before swapping numbers with Sia. Even though Arley's summer at home was over and she'd be returning to school, meeting Sia felt more like a beginning. Emma, on the other hand, wasn't sure if her conversation with Xavier was an ending or the start of a new chapter of stress.

"How do you feel about all this, Charles? Because you're part of this equation now. I don't want you to feel uncomfortable."

"Emma, I'd be comfortable if it was just me and you standing in the rain on the side of Langston Road. As long as I am with you."

"You know, that is how we met!" Emma laughed.

They each said in unison, "Looking for Poppy!"

"Am I making a mistake?" Emma asked. "Forgiving the unforgivable?"

"From my vantage point forgiveness isn't something you're giving to Xavier. It's the permission you're giving yourself to let go of a lot of pain."

"I'm so tired of carrying around the past. I just need a soft place to land. It feels that way when I'm around you," she said, her eyes studying Charles. "You have a pretty good last name, too. I'm thinking about taking it."

"Oh, are you now?"

"Emma Hodges. It just sounds *good!*" Her southern speak stretched out the word *good* like she was tearing apart a warm, gooey sugar cookie.

"But is it worth paying all that money for a name change? You're still you, no matter what your last name is."

"Oh, Charles, we worked all of that out, remember? It's much cheaper if we just get married. That was your idea."

"Yes, it was, Emma. Yes, it was."

And with that, standing on the soft grassy lawn beside the Roscoe statue, Charles and Emma chose their wedding date. They'd marry in December when, as Emma put it, the trees would already be lit for the holidays and the tax break would go into effect before the new year. Charles knew he was marrying a businessperson, and Emma knew she was marrying her soft place to land.

CHAPTER 14

Hope

Time moves differently for a dog, especially the closer time ticks toward the end. In their final hours, animals stay in the present, unaware that their time could run out. They're not thinking about what comes next as much as what's happening now. It's simple: They are comfortable or not. Their human is with them or not. Life is present or...not. People, on the other hand, mark each moment, counting birthdays and anniversaries, doctor visits and medical treatments. Loss, and the potential for it, hangs heavy over the human psyche. When faced with the threat of mortality, fear floods human senses. People grab onto hope like a raft and cling tightly as life flows faster and faster and faster beyond control, hoping for a change in current. Hope, after all, is among humanity's greatest gifts, awarded to compensate for the pain of enduring a lifespan over several decades in which we could—and do—lose those closest to us. How would anyone survive life without hope? It distracts from the inevitable and fuels the fight to preserve life at all costs, even if just for one more day.

Animals don't need it. An animal's ability to marry their thoughts to the present is one of their greatest gifts, granted as compensation for an unjustly shorter lifespan than humans. Their minds remain anchored in the moment, feeling the joy or pain of the present, and blissfully unaware that their time on earth cannot tick beyond their teenage years. To a dog, life lasts as long as their love—forever. Who needs hope when you have forever? For people, a dog's life—no matter the years—lasts long enough to break their hearts when it ends. The entire process is enough to think there's nothing divine in this world because the loss is so unfair. Then, there's love—all that love. How could we ever doubt it? Hope is all we've got.

Roscoe never fretted over his own mortality. In the eight years he spent roaming the mountains as a stray, he never feared death. For the seven years after that, after finding his home the community center, he only felt loved. Fear didn't enter his mind when he hurt his leg along the roadside, or when his limp persisted for weeks afterwards, and certainly not during the last twelve painful days after his statue debuted. The dog just hurt. Yet the fear of losing Roscoe never left J.D.'s mind. He hoped the dog's lethargic behavior since the unveiling was nothing more than the byproduct of all the excitement from so many visitors on campus.

"He's just tired," J.D. hoped.

In the twelve days since the statue was revealed, Roscoe changed his routine. He stopped making his rounds from the cafeteria to the softball field. Instead, he slept late in J.D.'s office and then limped outside around noon to sit in the sun. Each day, visitors petted his head and posed for selfies with him. Each day, after a couple of hours with his fans, he would retreat into air-conditioned comfort. Each day, he limped inside a little earlier. J.D. hoped it was from overstimulation. He hoped it was the heat. He hoped.

J.D. hoped even on the day he was unable to locate the dog when it was time to go home. Roscoe wasn't sitting on his corduroy dog bed. He wasn't in the conference room by the air vent, either. Or under his desk. He wasn't in any of his usual places.

"*Odd*," J.D. said to himself, as he messaged Darrell to join him on a quick cross-campus Roscoe search. He picked J.D. up on a golf cart, and they began their sweep all around campus. They went to each of Roscoe's haunts—from the spot in the gymnasium where he'd nap on rainy days to the computer lab where he'd snuggle by the feet of someone using a computer. He wasn't in any of the usual places, not even his spot outside the window to the kitchen cafeteria where he'd catch scraps thrown his way from the cook. Darrell and J.D. searched until the sunset cast long, late-summer shadows. Roscoe was nowhere to be found.

"Go on home, Darrell. It's getting late," said J.D. "Maybe Roscoe will wander back in when he's ready."

"I hate to leave you alone when we don't know where the ol' boy is hiding."

"He'll turn up. He always comes home."

The only thing left for J.D. to do was wait back in his office. He walked across campus alone as dusk arrived. As he entered the glass doors to the administration building, he heard a scurrying sound in his office.

"Roscoe?"

"It's just me!" Patty called out. "Did you find Roscoe?"

"No, did you?" J.D. said. "Wait, how did you know he's missing?"

"Oh, Darrell texted all of us to be on the lookout. I've been trying to find him, too."

"This isn't like him."

Thud. Thud. Thud.

A kicking sound was coming from the back door to the administration building, like someone or something was trying to get in. J.D. and Patty ran down the long hall, through the conference room, and to the metal door. A thick bar across it warned that an alarm would sound if it opened, since it's only to be used in case of emergency.

Thud. Thud. Thud.

"Should we open it?" Patty asked. "Sounds like someone is out there kicking on the door."

"It could be Roscoe," J.D. said, his heart too filled with hope to realize that, since the accident, the old dog's legs haven't been strong enough to kick anything, much less something metal.

He pushed open the emergency door, which made a scraping sound against the concrete outside.

Bzzzzzzzzz. Bzzzzzzzzz. Bzzzzzzzzz.

As the alarm blared, Patty and J.D. gasped at what they saw. Standing in the yellow light of the streetlamp was Xavier. In his arms, cradled like a baby, was the heavy Lab. They both appeared to be in pain. Xavier rushed past J.D. and Patty, straining to carry the heavy dog into the building.

Bzzzzzzzzz. Bzzzzzzzzz.

"I promise I didn't do this. I promise, I promise, I promise," he said. "Where can I put him? Somewhere soft?"

"His bed is in my office, Xavier," said J.D., his voice calm but his eyes full of questions. Patty ran to try to turn off the blaring alarm.

"It's his legs," Xavier said. "They aren't working."

Bzzzzzzzzz. Bzzzzzzzzz.

The alarm kept blaring and J.D. thought he misheard Xavier.

"What do you mean, his legs aren't working?"

Roscoe's brown eyes locked on J.D. as Xavier lowered him to the ground. He watched his person intently. J.D. knew he was in pain from his expression. The dog swapped his signature slobbery smile for a serious stare, as though Roscoe was saying "Something is wrong."

Bzzzzzzzzz. Bzzzzzzzzz.

"I can't think right with that alarm," J.D. said.

"I'm trying to figure it out!" yelled Patty.

"I found him outside the softball field," Xavier explained. "I was finishing my grounds work when he just sort of crawled out of the shrubbery."

"Crawled out?" J.D. asked.

"More like dragged than crawled," Xavier said. "He's hurt. I swear I just found him; I didn't do anything."

Bzzzzzzzz. Bzzz—

"I got it! The alarm's off!" Patty announced.

J.D. bent over and rubbed Roscoe's coarse black fur from his head down to his back. As he neared the tops of his rear legs, Roscoe grew tense and clenched his body in pain. J.D. examined each leg, searching for a cut or a break. He found no sign of injury.

"I think maybe he lost control of his backside," Xavier said. "The way he was moving, it was like his front legs were pulling his hind legs through the grass. That's what I meant by dragging. He wasn't walking on four legs; he was dragging himself by his front two."

"I'll call Charles and Emma," Patty said. "A house call from his vet will get Roscoe good as new."

"Roscoe, are you hurt, boy?" J.D. asked, laying down on the office floor beside him. "Can you move?"

They stared into each other's eyes face-to-face, the dog's filled with pain and the human's filled with worry. J.D. gently massaged Roscoe's scalp. The Lab relaxed his ears and seemed to appreciate the relief. As J.D. moved his hand down his spine, he pressed firmly with his fingers the way Roscoe always liked.

He could almost make out a slight smile on the dog's lips until his hand got down toward Roscoe's back legs. There was no expression of pain or relief. Not when J.D. moved his right rear leg, or his left one. Not when he tapped the bottom of his foot. Not even when he lifted the dog's heavy hip. Roscoe didn't even react when J.D. gently pinched the dog's ankle. Not even a flinch. The problem was that the dog didn't seem to feel anything in his rear legs. J.D. slowly stood and turned toward Xavier.

"Thank you for bringing him to me, Xavier. You should call it a night now."

"I promise I did nothing to hurt him, J.D. You believe me, right? I know you must be thinking I did something to him, but I promised I've changed. If I had hurt him, I wouldn't have brought him back here."

"I don't know what happened to Roscoe," J.D. said. "And since I don't know, I don't blame you for it. Some folks are coming to look after him and I think it's best if you aren't around when they get here. But I thank you for bringing him to us."

"Of course," Xavier said, as he walked toward the door, Xavier turned to look back at the dog.

"Bye, Roscoe," he said, pulling his cap down from his head. "I hope you feel much better in the morning."

Roscoe watched him leave, then turned his eyes back toward J.D., who hadn't stopped examining his dog.

"Want me to leave, too?" Patty asked. "You and Roscoe may want some time to yourself."

"It's okay, Patty. You're family. You need time with Roscoe as much as me. He'll feel better with you here."

"I need to call Bell," said J.D. "She'll want to know."

"I already texted her."

Within a few minutes, Bell arrived with steak sliders for J.D., Patty, and one for Roscoe, too. It was his favorite of all the treats ever slipped his way, but on this night, he turned his head at the sight of it. Soon, Charles and Emma joined the crew. Charles carried his medical bag with all the supplies he'd need to perform an examination, and Emma carried a small pouch with gemstones to help Roscoe heal.

"It's clear quartz and amethyst. These got me through my dental surgery," she said as she placed the gemstones around his corduroy bed. "They'll help him, too."

For the next hour, Charles listened to Roscoe's heart, monitored the dog's breathing, and seemed to examine every piece of fur from his head to tail. Bell kept trying to tempt the dog with the steak slider. She hoped filling his belly may give him the strength needed to move his legs, but he wouldn't take a bite. Emma rubbed the green worry stone in her pocket. J.D. didn't say a word. Instead, he watched. He thought. He waited. And he soothed Roscoe, nuzzling the dog's forehead from his seat on the floor beside him.

"J.D., could I talk to you," Charles asked. "Back there?"

He pointed to the conference room as Emma and Bell looked at each other. They knew only one reason Charles would ask J.D. to talk away from them, and it wasn't good.

"J.D., I don't think this is an injury. I think it's nerve damage," Charles explained. "He doesn't seem to have been hurt by anything external."

"That's good, right?" J.D. asked. "He isn't hurt?"

"Well, not externally. I think the problem may be something internal. I think, maybe, it's a nerve connected to his spine. Now, it could just be pinched. I hope that's the case. But it's more than likely severed. In that case, Roscoe would never walk again."

"I see. So, what would we do then?"

"Well, again, let's hope it's pinched. I'm going to give him some medicine, with your consent, of course. It will relax him and loosen up the muscles.

If it's pinched, some sensation will return in a few hours. Either way, I'd like for you to bring him in for an X-Ray tomorrow morning, so we know for sure."

"Of course. But what if it's severed?"

"Well, J.D. then it may be time to make a tough decision."

"You mean—" J.D. couldn't say it.

"He'd need you to make the choice. Dogs are tough. Some of them go quickly and some can hang on like this for a long time—suffering."

"We could carry him wherever he needed to go," J.D. said.

"You could."

"Or maybe build him a cart for him with the wheels on the back so he could move around."

"You could."

"Maybe we could even build a path for him, to make it easier to roll himself through campus."

"You could do all those things, J.D. But he'd suffer. As his vet, I'd suggest you look at three key indicators when considering what's the best treatment for him: Can he walk? Can he go to the bathroom on his own? Can he eat?"

"Right now, he can't do any of those things," J.D. said.

"Let's give him the medicine, and see what tomorrow brings, J.D. He's a very special dog. I'll do everything I can for him, you know that."

"I know you will."

After administering the medication to Roscoe, Charles, and Emma each gave the dog a kiss on the head and went home. Patty left, too, promising to keep everyone at the community center updated so J.D. could focus on the dog. With the lights dimmed in his office, he laid beside the black Lab, who was relentlessly watching him.

"Bell, could I have one of those steak sandwiches?" J.D. asked.

"Sure," she said, "Let me heat it up for you in the break room."

"No, it's okay. It's not for me," he explained.

He took the slider and removed the bun, then chewed up the steak so it was very fine and practically shredded.

"Don't watch me, Bell. I'm about to spit this out."

"Does it taste bad?" Bell asked.

As he took the meat out of his mouth, J.D. pressed it against Roscoe's teeth like a bird feeding its baby.

"Here, boy. Just eat, please. Eat something," he said.

"Oh, J.D." Bell said, her heart heavy from the determined love she saw J.D. pour on to his dog.

"It's just too tough for him to chew. If I can get the meat fine enough, he'll be able to swallow it. If he eats, he'll get stronger. Then maybe he can walk and go to the bathroom on his own. Charles said that's all he needs to do—eat, walk, and go to the bathroom."

It was no use. Roscoe wouldn't bite the steak, no matter how soft and chewy. For the rest of the night J.D. laid on the floor beside him, as Bell texted worried updates to Charles and Emma. By midnight, the medicine relaxed the dog and J.D. could hear him snoring ever so slightly. That sound soothed him and he wrapped his arm around Roscoe's thick body and gently rocked his dog. Somewhere, between hope and worry, J.D. drifted to sleep, too. When he opened his eyes, he felt Roscoe's heavy head resting on his chest. The dog had crawled on top of him, and his body laid on J.D. like a weighted blanket. J.D. could feel the canine's slow breath move in and out, but his body was flat and almost lifeless. As the sun rose outside, J.D. tried to align his own breathing with Roscoe's. He resisted the urge to wake him to see if maybe, just maybe, he was walking again. Had the medicine worked? Would he eat steak for breakfast?

But instead of rushing, he just waited. He laid in the moment—present, saving his worry for later, as he savored the experience of feeling his dog on his chest. The minutes moved differently for J.D., and he wanted to savor them—just in case. He stroked Roscoe's forehead, running his fingers behind his floppy ear, and gently squeezed his arms together in a deep hug. He waited. And waited. And waited. But Roscoe never moved. Not even when he called Bell over to tempt him with fresh steak, treats, cheese and every doggy delicacy stored in his office. He didn't move. He didn't eat.

"Roscoe, it's time to wake up, boy. Want to go see your statue?" J.D. asked.

Roscoe opened his eyes and stared at him. For a moment the dog smiled at J.D. He wasn't expecting to wake up on his person's chest, but as quickly as the smile formed, his face twisted into a look of concern. He began to wiggle and move awkwardly. He appeared to be trying to stand.

"That's it, Roscoe! You can do it. You can get up and walk!" J.D. cheered him on.

But Roscoe could not stand. When he shifted weight to his front legs, he slipped, unable to move his back legs to catch himself. As J.D. rose to stabilize him, Roscoe lost control of his back half all together, and a puddle began growing under him. He'd been unable to hold it any longer. The urine pooled around his legs and the dog was stuck, unknowingly dragging his feet through the wetness on the floor, unable to move away from the flow.

"Oh, Roscoe, I'm so sorry boy." J.D. said. "We'll clean you up."

All four of Roscoe's legs seemed to give out at once. He couldn't walk. He couldn't eat. He couldn't go to the bathroom on his own.

"Charles will know how to fix this," J.D. hoped.

They wrapped the old dog in a blue blanket—the one with Trooper the mustang embroidered on the trim—and, together, loaded him into their SUV. Once at the clinic, Charles ran the X-ray, which confirmed what he'd feared. Roscoe's nerve had severed, and it paralyzed him from the waist down. At his age, the strain of pulling his heavy body would be too much for his front legs, which suffered from arthritis and bone density loss. As Charles reviewed the scans, he assured J.D. that the damage was unavoidable.

"There's no one to blame, J.D. It's genetics. This isn't from an injury or an accident. This is from a long, happy life. His body just can't keep up with his spirit," Charles said. "He won't heal from this."

"Could Bell and I have a minute alone with him?"

"Of course," Charles said. "Take all the time you need. The clinic is yours today."

Time moves differently for a human, when the inevitable arrives and the thing they hoped wouldn't happen comes to be. Minutes stand as still as hours as all the distractions of the world fade. Nothing else matters. Nothing except the choice ahead.

"How do I know when it's time, Bell? It's never going to feel right."

"Only you know. Only you," she said. "You'll know when."

"I can't bear the thought of...hurting him."

"No one has cared for him like you. He knows that. Letting go is caring for him, J.D. It's the most selfless act we can ever make for our pets. The choice you're making is to endure your own heartache in exchange for relieving his suffering."

"I don't want him to suffer," J.D. said, his voice cracking. His hope now was that he'd know when the moment was right to begin the procedure to help Roscoe move on.

In the stillness of the empty clinic, Roscoe opened his eyes and gazed directly at J.D. Even a small movement made him grimace with pain. But the dog seemed determined to deliver his message. Without saying a word, J.D. felt Roscoe tell him "*It's okay*" with those big brown eyes. For J.D. that moment changed "*How can I do this?*" to "*How could I not?*" No creature, especially one as unique as his Roscoe, deserved to suffer. Charles entered the room with another vet. Charles was too connected to Roscoe to perform the procedure himself, but he wanted to oversee it to make sure the dog felt as comfortable as he could.

"Will you want to stay in the room with him?" he asked.

J.D. didn't answer, unaware there was any other option. To him, there was no choice. Any pet deserves their person there, no matter how hard it is to watch. While their lives may be shorter, their person is the center of their world.

"J.D.?"

"Of course."

"Most pet owners say it's too hard to watch."

"How could I leave him alone now?" He placed his hand over Roscoe's chest. "I'll be right here. Till the end."

Charles dimmed the lights and played soothing music to help relax Roscoe. Emma had already placed salt rock lamps and gemstones in each corner of the room, which smelled like sage from incense smoldering in the corner.

"It will help him transition," she said.

Emma and Charles held hands as the other vet began the process. Bell stood stoically, her hand on J.D.'s shoulder, her own heart aching for him, for Roscoe...and for the other beloved pets she'd helped cross over when their bodies failed their spirit. All that loss and love flowed around her.

"We'll begin now," the vet stated, but it sounded more like a question. J.D. nodded his head in agreement and held his breath.

First came an injection to relax the canine. Almost instantly, Roscoe's tense expression relaxed. On the outside, he appeared younger and at ease in a way J.D. hadn't seen him in years. On the inside, Roscoe sensed so much more than the pain. In fact, any trace of it already began fading away as the medicine distanced him from it. Roscoe's mind filled with explorations across the pine-coated woods, drinking from the stream that flows down the mountain, the cool breeze on his ears during golf cart rides with J.D., countless treats from his many visitors and those smiles—those magical and wonderous expressions from people that tell animals they are safe, loved, and wanted. At that moment, a lifetime of love washed over Roscoe like a wave breaking onto shore. It flowed and flowed and flowed until there was no discomfort for the dog, not now, only separation from the constraints of mortality and the end of his pain. For J.D., who kept his hand on

Roscoe's chest until the gentle rise and fall of his breath slowed still, there was no relief, just loss.

"Goodbye, Roscoe," he said. "I'll never forget you."

J.D. hoped he made the right decision—not one day early or one day too late.

CHAPTER 15

Sacred Harp Songs

Flash. Flash. Flash.

From the driver's seat of Bell's SUV, sunlight cut through tall pines like a strobe light. The trees lined the road on both sides and soothed her as their branches filtered the light along Langston Road. It was an unusual morning for her as J.D.'s chauffeur. Usually he drove himself to work, taking the shortcut along Langston Gap Road with its dangerous curves and crumbling asphalt. Bell insisted if she was driving today, they'd take the safer, scenic route along the river.

Flash. Flash. Flash.

For a fraction of a second, each of the tall trunks blocked the bright sun twinkling from the other side of the branches. The rapid contrast of dark to light flickered in a hypnotic glow as Bell drove J.D. to work the day after Roscoe died. She'd left her car at the community center the night before, and even if she hadn't, she didn't want J.D. to be alone when he returned to his office without the dog that had greeted him every day. J.D. stared out of the passenger window, his eyes tracking the white line on the side of the road. In the wash of the bright yellow light, he felt nothing...but also everything. After choosing the unimaginable for his pet, there was a fine line between relief and devastation. In his grief, uncertainty reared its head. For the first time since he'd taken the job of director at the community center, he was unsure how to move forward.

"What will I tell everyone?"

"What do you mean, J.D.?"

"They'll want to know what happened."

"I have a feeling everyone knows. News travels fast around here, especially about Roscoe."

"But will they be upset that I—" he paused.

"That you what, J.D.?"

"That I didn't save him. People may be upset with me."

Flash! Flash! Flash!

As they drove over a narrow causeway, there were no trees to block the sun. Light beams reflecting off the lake on each side of them exploded like a mirror ball as Bell looked at him.

"No one is going to be upset with you. They are upset *for* you," she said.

"I'm the one who is supposed to be there for them."

"Community is a two-way street, J.D. Let them carry you through this."

"It just seems selfish when so many people have gone through so much worse."

"Loss is loss, J.D."

The drive to work seemed to never end, and the pain of losing Roscoe merged with a sense of dread building in his chest as he thought about walking in his office and seeing the empty dog bed. When he arrived with Bell at his side, there was very little to see. The entire administration building seemed empty. Patty wasn't in her office. Lynde wasn't at her desk. No volunteers walked around the grounds, yet every space in the parking lot was filled.

"This is strange," said J.D., taking a deep breath before stepping into his office, expecting to face the empty dog bed. But it was missing, too. In its place was a folded note, with the letters *"J.D."* written in calligraphy on the front flap. Inside the message read *"Meet us by the walking trail."*

"What's going on, Bell?"

"I don't know, but let's go to the trail."

They cut through the back hall, passed the empty computer labs, and crossed the rear parking lot, which was also filled with cars. As they stepped out onto the grassy field behind the center, they could hear voices, chanting softly as first.

"*Fa-fa-fa. Sol-la. Fa-fa-fa. Sol-la.*"

The chorus crescendoed as the crowd noticed J.D. and Bell approaching.

"*Fa-sol. La-mi. Fa-sol. La-mi.*"

J.D.'s heart raced with both surprise and intrigue.

"It sounds like shape note music!" he said.

"Sacred Harp?" Bell asked.

"Yes, like my grandfather used to sing."

When J.D. was a child, Sand Mountain musicians performed sacred harp singing, also known as shape note music. Its other-worldly sound stretched back deep in the antebellum roots of Appalachian history. Shape note music gave untrained singers a way to sing from the crumpled pages of post-Civil War hymnals at a time many of them struggled to read. They didn't need to know the words if they could read the "fa sol la" notes written in the music. The a cappella tradition was passed down generation to generation, stopping mostly around the time J.D. first heard it as a young boy at his Grandfather Jink's funeral. Now, as a seasoned man with academic accolades lining the walls of his office, the music born from those who struggled to read a book somehow expressed more about the loss he felt than any words he could find.

"Fa-fa-sol. La-la-mi. Fa-sol-la-mi."

The choir grew louder and louder as its sound swelled with sorrow, joy, and as much Southern tradition as deviled eggs at a church picnic. The melody enchanted J.D., who found himself carried by the shape note music as he and Bell walked closer and closer to the group gathered near the walking trail. At the gravel entrance, rows of community members lined each side of the path. They stood shoulder to shoulder, people were as numerous as the pine trees lining Langston Road.

"Fa-fa-sol. La-la-mi. Fa-sol-la-mi."

The song carried J.D. down the path to the pond, where he was surrounded by those who had heard the news of Roscoe's death and came to the community center to offer their condolences. He saw faces he'd missed for years, and others he recognized from ordinary daily interactions. There was Kramer from the gym and the clerk at Hammers Department Store. He saw Hunter from of The *Sentinel* and the young man who cut the grass at the Rec-Com in Scottsboro. Darrell's wife, Berdie, waved at him, her arm around their boy Derrick. Vann, David, and Norman stood together beside the golf cart they'd driven so many times with Roscoe on board. Laura and Becky arrived fresh from their beach vacation with Liz, her face sun-kissed pink beneath her best wide brim hat. Andrea's voice cut through the crowd, catching his attention even before he saw her compassionate smile. He spotted Clyde from Red Bucks and, for a moment, he even thought he saw his dear friend Ronnie, who didn't live long enough to see him run the community center, but who would have been his biggest fan.

As J.D. felt so many palms pressing against his back, he didn't notice the emotion rolling down his face—a sacred release reserved only for the most meaningful of moments. As he neared the end of the trail, Emma and Charles waved from beside a mound of rocks arranged in an intricate formation. The rocks curved along the ground toward a circle in which a row of stones spun into itself. It looked like a whirlpool made out of rocks. On the other side of the formation Patty, Brenda, Trish, and the rest of the crew from the J.D.C. Day celebrations gathered, singing along with the sound of sacred harp. Even though he'd never sung shape note before, J.D. belted out along with the crowd in a cathartic chant of *"Fa-fa-sol. La-la-mi. Fa-sol-la-mi."* Their voices combined as one, echoing across the pond at the center of the walking trail. Slowly, the crowd lining the path closed inward and formed a circle around the rocky mound.

"Is this what I think it is?" J.D. asked.

"We prepared it early this morning," Patty explained. "A final resting place for the finest Lab we've ever known."

"Thank you," J.D. said. "I didn't know where to bury him. This is the spot."

Roscoe's grave sat on the field at the top of the trail. It was the most peaceful clearing on campus, made even more sacred with the elaborate design written in stone. The rocks formed an infinity symbol, wrapping around the grave.

"Barbara designed it," Patty explained. "It was only right, since she designed his statue."

"It's perfect. Just perfect," he said. "How did you do this so quickly?"

"You can thank him for the labor," she said, pointing to a man in a red flannel shirt.

Alone in the back of the crowd, his bearded face was still dirt-stained from digging into Alabama red clay and then hauling several hundred pounds of rock to the gravesite. Xavier removed his hat and bowed his head down in respect. J.D. waved to him before he disappeared among all the other familiar faces.

"I decided I'd forgive him," Patty said. "He started working on this at dawn."

"How did he know?"

"Well...you can thank Emma for that."

Emma sighed as she gave Patty a mean side eye.

"Look, J.D. He owed me one. And I decided what better way for me to collect than to help you."

"Thank you, Emma. I know that wasn't an easy call to make."

"I know you had a hard choice to make, too. We do what we have to do, J.D."

"Mr. J.D.," a voice called up, as he felt a tug at his shirttail. He looked down to see Anna, holding a single camellia bloom in her hand. "I'm so sorry for your loss. I loved him, too."

"Thank you, Anna. I know you did. And he loved you. He loved everyone here."

Anna placed the pink bloom on top of the mound, followed by Lilah, then Patty, then Emma...then dozens of others who placed their flower on the grave.

"This...is incredible," J.D. said to Bell. "He was so loved."

"*You* are so loved," she said.

Bell placed the last flower over the memorial, as J.D. turned to address the crowd.

"Words fail to express what this means to me, but I know you all feel that connection I do right now. I could hear it in your voices as you sang the notes of our ancestors. *Fa-sol-la* meant *"I love you"* and *Sol-la mi* said, *"I'm here for you."* I needed that, just like I needed Roscoe. We all needed that dog. We didn't choose him. He chose us. We wouldn't have it any other way. And while we'd never choose to part with him, or with anyone we love, I now stand with a sense of relief that he isn't suffering...and that he'll always be home in this beautiful memorial. Thank you for this gift."

For the next half hour, maybe an hour, or maybe even longer, J.D. stayed at the memorial and talked to everyone who approached him, thanking them for honoring Roscoe.

"We were just here a couple of weeks ago," one visitor said. "For the statue dedication. I'm so glad he lived to see that."

Another complimented the beautiful floral blanket someone had draped over the statue, adding a colorful cape to both Trooper and Roscoe's lookalikes.

And yet another asked a question that sent J.D. and the rest of his friends back to the heart of campus to see whatever had been left at the statue. The question was *"Who do you think left out all of that money?"*

Beside the statue, between the mustang's long legs and the black Lab's broad shoulders, someone had placed a clear plastic bin on the ground with the words "Roscoe Scholarship" handwritten in black ink. On top, it contained a small slit wide enough to slide a dollar bill inside, but instead of dollar bills the bin filled with tens, twenties and at least a couple of hundred-dollar bills.

"Who left this out here?" J.D. asked.

No one knew.

"Standby!" Patty called up, pulling up the campus livestream on her cell phone. She scrolled back, scanning the video in reverse as person after person approached the bin.

Emma, Charles, Bell, and J.D. all watched with curious anticipation for the good Samaritan to be revealed.

"Hurry, Patty! I've got to know who did this!" Emma called out.

"Almost there," Patty said, her finger ferociously scrolling back through the footage. "It only looks like it has a few dollars in it now. I'm almost to the start of it."

Their answer was captured in video pixels. A man in red flannel left the donation bin beside the statue. A man who just a few months before had antagonized the sweet ol' Lab was now raising money in his memory.

"Well, I didn't have that on my bingo card!" Emma blurted out.

"Someone bring Xavier here," J.D. said calmly. "We need to talk."

"I'm here," Xavier shouted. He'd been watching from beneath the awning outside the cafeteria to make sure no one tried to steal any of the donation money. As he stepped down the campus sidewalk, he may as well have been strolling the perp walk behind the county jail. His face looked as guilty as if he'd stolen all that money instead of raised it.

Emma clasped Charles' hand tightly, her eyes open wide in anticipation of what might happen.

"You okay?" Charles whispered to her.

"All good, baby. I just wish I had some popcorn to snack on during all of this drama. What do you think is about to go down?"

"Well, I—"

"Shhh," she hushed him. "We don't want to miss this."

With J.D. beside the bronze Lab and Xavier next to the tall mustang, the two men looked each other square in the eyes. The bin stuffed with money sat on the ground between them.

"You did this?" J.D. asked.

"Yessir."

"Why?"

"Well," Xavier looked down. "I made some mistakes with your dog. Real big mistakes. I've always regretted that. Especially since I've volunteered out here. Your dog never held those bad things against me. I guess Roscoe helped me understand what it's like to fit in somewhere."

"I don't blame you for what happened to him, Xavier. You didn't kill him. It was genetic."

"I hope that's true," Xavier said. "But I kept thinking of something you said at the statue dedication: A bad thing happened and then something wonderful happened. I wanted to do something that was a part of the wonderful—and not just the bad for a change. I hope this money helps do that."

"You know, Xavier. Roscoe was a street dog before he chose us here at the community center. We really had to watch him those first few months. Sometimes he'd act like he was going to bite. He'd growl. He'd snarl. He made a few folks nervous," J.D.

said. "But after spending enough time out here, that softened up. I'd even say it got tamed out of him."

"I didn't know that about Roscoe."

They both found their eyes drawn to the bronze statue immortalizing the dog.

"I think you and Roscoe had a lot more in common than you realize," said J.D.

"What do you think changed him?" Xavier asked.

"He found a home."

"Oh, it was a little more than that," Patty said. She joined the two of them by the statue. "A lot of people said Roscoe hung out with J.D. so much that he took all the rough stuff out of him. He gave Roscoe a different way of seeing humans."

"We treat everyone the same out here," J.D. said. "No matter where you come from or what you did. We're equal, as long as you treat everyone else with respect. And I mean everyone."

Xavier nodded, knowingly.

"Do you understand, Xavier? Everyone."

Patty and Bell looked toward one another. They anticipated what would come next after the comparison J.D. made between Roscoe and Xavier. As a former teacher, it was in J.D.'s DNA to share life lessons through comparison. Emma, on the other hand, anticipated something different. She elbowed Charles, her eyes locked on the two men beside the statue, and whispered "Did you hear that, Charles? J.D. is about to let him have it."

"I don't know, Emma. That's not really his style."

"Shhh, I don't want to miss this!"

Emma's eyes widened as she shook her head and turned to Charles.

"I'm sorry, honey. I didn't mean to shush you! That was rude."

"It's okay, Emma." Charles said. "I'm kind of wanting some popcorn myself!"

J.D. put his hand on the bronze statue over Roscoe's chest, just as he had the day before in the vet's office.

"You know," J.D. said. "I like how you were thinking by raising that donation money, Xavier. Something terrible happened, but something good can happen, too. I think we'll use this money to start a new class out here."

"I like the sound of that, J.D. Something good for the community."

"But what should we teach?" He asked, as he looked over at Patty. "I'm thinking entrepreneurship.

Something that will help people make their dreams a reality."

"Like how you paid for the Roscoe statue with snack machine money!" Patty added. "That's entrepreneurship! The ability to make things happen."

He tapped the statue on top of Roscoe's forehead, just like he used to do for the real dog.

"Entrepreneurship is a fitting topic for the first thing to come from the Roscoe scholarship," J.D. said.

"I'm glad you can put that money to use," Xavier said, extending his hand to J.D. for a quick handshake. He nervously straightened his red flannel shirt, aware that he was in the center of attention. "I should get going now. You nice folks deserve some time together."

As he turned his back to J.D. and stepped away, Xavier felt a hand on his shoulder.

"One more thing before you go," he said.

"I'll do anything you need. Want me to clean up down by the trail?"

"I want you to be here when I announce something."

J.D. huddled with Lynde, who seemed to be helping him calculate something on her phone. After she nodded her head in support of whatever J.D. was proposing, he raised his hand to get the attention of the dozen or so people still at the center after the memorial service. As they gathered around the Roscoe statue, he explained what Xavier had done to collect donations for the scholarship.

"Patty, what are our options for a donation such as this?"

"Well, we could wait and think and let this money sit unused," she said. "Or we could start doing some good today."

"Let's do that," he said. "I'm proud to announce the first recipient of the Roscoe Scholarship, covering all costs associated with our soon-to-be-launched entrepreneurial certification will be...Xavier Johnson."

The announcement landed so unexpectedly, Xavier would have been less surprised to see the Roscoe statue jump to life and the bronze Lab lick him on the face. Charles and Emma appeared equally shocked by the news. Emma's eyes swelled in size, glistening as they pooled with tears of.... Anger? Sadness? Missed opportunity? Resentment? Loss? As all of it swirled inside her, but on the outside she smiled softly and said "Congratulations, Xavier."

He nodded his head. The crowd looked as though they expected some sort of acceptance speech, but words failed him. His crippling sense of imposter syndrome made it worse. He heard his father's voice screaming in his head, *"You don't deserve this."* As Xavier looked at the faces with their expectations of a speech, he locked on to Emma. He felt like he was stealing something that belonged to her.

Charles tightly squeezed Emma's hand. He felt all of it, too, by proxy. Anger. Sadness. Resentment. After all of Emma's years in business for herself, how could J.D. not have thought of her? Without Emma's business plan, Charles knew he would never have been able to open their clinic. All of it felt so unjust to him as, once again, Xavier seemed to get the better of Emma. How could this man steal an opportunity from a woman so deserving, just by donating other people's money?

"Xavier, the one condition is you have to uphold our high standards of respect for all—that includes people and animals. And when you're able, teach what you learn to someone else."

"You have my word," Xavier said. "I'll be honest, J.D. I'm not what I want to be, but I'm where I need to be to get there. Thank you for taking a chance on me."

Xavier's eyes pooled with gratitude, as he envisioned how differently his life may have been if he'd had a father like J.D., who somehow balanced opportunity, accountability, and kindness.

"There's one more thing," J.D told the group, refocusing their attention back to him.

"There's always one more thing," Patty whispered to Bell. "That's my rule number eleven of working with J.D. You've got to stay ready for the "one more thing" because it's usually the best thing!"

"We're going to need someone to lead this program," J.D. said. "Someone with first-hand experience, leadership, a track record of success. This program should help our community turn a scrappy idea into a community sensation. They need to know every aspect of starting your own business—from how to manage social media to ensuring everyone who completes the program is inclusive in our community."

Snap. Snap. Snap. Snap.

Patty snapped her fingers, her arm held high over her head as she shouted out, "That's right, J.D. After all, the Roscoe statue represents acceptance of all—no matter your differences. All means all, y'all!"

"There's really only one person for this job. The question is will she accept it?" J.D. stepped over toward Emma and asked, "Will you lead the program, Emma?"

Again, all the emotions welled up inside her. Surprise. Excitement. Accomplishment. She'd waited so long to feel pride in someone other than her child or in something other than her business. In this moment, she felt pride for herself. The anger and resentment that swirled fervently just before melted away as quickly as an ice cube on a front porch floor as Emma realized she wouldn't be a student in the class, she'd be the teacher building it. She loved creating new things, especially to help others. The new job would demand a new level of interaction with Xavier as her first student, and for an instant that terrified her. Then, a confidence took over as Emma realized she'd be in a position of authority over Xavier. He couldn't ruin this opportunity for her or for anyone. It gave her power. She stepped toward J.D. to shake his hand, but the handshake became a hug.

"I don't hug!" She shouted, wiping her glistening cheek, "And I don't cry. But...there's just a lot happening today!"

"Is that a yes?"

"Yes! Yes! I accept, J.D. Whole-heartedly. Thank you."

"It's a yes!" Patty shouted out.

"One thing though," Emma said.

"There's always one thing with Emma," Charles whispered to Bell. "And it's usually the most important part!"

"I won't be stepping away from my gemstone store or my partnership at the clinic with Charles. Those are my forevers," she said. "Is that okay?"

"Of course," J.D. said. "This will be a part-time program. You can develop it however and whenever you want. In fact, consider this your down payment to get started."

He handed her the donation bin, overflowing with donations.

"Well, I didn't have *this* on my bingo card, either!" She laughed. "But I like it. Just call me Professor! Thank you for trusting me, J.D. I promise, I won't let you down."

"Oh, I *know* you won't Emma."

"How can you be so sure? I've never taught a class before."

"Because you are...*you.*"

Friends and visitors lingered around the community center until the shadows grew long. As is tradition in the South, people had brought casseroles and cakes to soothe their friend's grief. They lingered, but what they were actually doing was checking on their person and staying by his side on this first full day without his Roscoe, just as he had been there for them on so many tough days in their own lives.

Losing a dog leaves more than a void in our heart. It also leaves an empty space in our time. Those instincts to fill the water bowl, to let them out for a walk, to call them inside at the end of the day...all the impulses of daily routine are like thorns of grief that prick your heart throughout a normal day and remind you of what's missing. Many of J.D.'s friends knew what was ahead, and they worried that without Roscoe, their leader may feel differently about spending as much time at the community center as had been his routine. Today marked the first day of living with the void.

At sunset, J.D. felt drawn to take one more stroll to the walking trail to view Roscoe's memorial, with Bell at his side. Together, they marveled at the design, the thoughtfulness and the significance of the infinity symbol embroidered in the ground in rock. When J.D. started his day, he was overwhelmed by the thought of burying his beloved pet. Thanks to friends and strangers from all different backgrounds, the burial was perfectly managed.

"They really know me," he said.

"They really love you," Bell added.

As the frogs croaked with the first hints of dusk, Bell gazed at the beautiful formation around her.

"Just look at this, J.D." she said as she stared at the memorial, built with a thousand small stones in just the right positions.

"With so much love," he said, "It's not goodbye. Not exactly. I'll never be without Roscoe out here. His legacy is everywhere."

"Just like yours," Bell said. "You two are forever intertwined."

"We all are."

CHAPTER 16

Something Borrowed

In the backseat, Arley Flores looked up from her phone for the first time during the entire hour-long ride home from the airport. She tried to focus on the scenery outside, as holiday lights twinkled and festive yard decorations sparkled vibrantly across snow-covered lawns. People around here made the holidays glitter, even if there wasn't much under the tree. Arley wanted to take in the magic, but she couldn't keep up with all the messages pinging on her phone. Every text she answered resulted in an almost-instant reply, like technological ping pong.

Ding. Ding.

Sia: OMG this is happening! Wait until you see my mom. She looks gorg.

Arley: I'm going to take so many pics!

Ding. Ding. Ding. Ding.

J.D.: Almost here? Bell and I are excited to see you!

Arley: Getting close! We're about to turn on Langston Gap Road. It's faster!

Bell: I'm not sure that's a good idea, Arley. That road is barely passable on a clear day.

Arley: I'm joking! If we slid off Langston Gap Road today, Emma would kill me!

Even the highway required careful navigation, with its icy coating on top of a surprise snowfall. Usually, these types of storms didn't hit between the mountains until at least January, but winter arrived early this year. Charles' joke was that Emma finally agreed to marry him on the day "hell froze over." Today, North Alabama did, too.

Ding. Ding.

Sia: If you're late because of the ice I'll totally stall the whole ceremony for you. Maybe I'll tell her we got engaged.

Arley: LOL. She'd just make it a double wedding!

As the car passed over Bob Jones Bridge, Arley tucked her long brown hair over her shoulder, then squeezed the two-studded aqua earrings she wore in her right ear, as she often did when she's anxious. Today's nerves were pure adrenaline. She'd flown in from Texas on a red-eye just a couple of hours after finishing finals. Her plane landed on schedule, but the passengers had to wait on the tarmac for an hour before they could deboard because the airport was so backed up due to three inches of snow. With the slick roads and blocked side streets, there was no time for Arley to go home and change clothes before Emma and Charles' commitment ceremony. Or, as most people would call it, their wedding. Emma preferred the term commitment ceremony because it seemed "more professional." Whatever she called it didn't matter to the couple's friends. Many had waited so long for this union, even a December snowstorm couldn't cool down the anticipation. In fact, as Arley stared out the window, the snow cast a beautiful "fresh start" coating over everything, adorning the pastures and farmhouses alongside the highway with a shimmering glaze. Despite the treacherous conditions, her driver seemed to be hyper focused on Arley's comfort.

"Doing okay back there? Need me to pull over so you can change?"

As Arley leaned forward to answer her driver, sunlight sparkled on the colorful gemstone jewelry wrapped around her neck and wrists. Sia had been mailing her trinkets from Emma's store every few weeks and, in return, Arley sent Sia hand-beaded Western jewelry she found in Austin's artisan shops. After Christmas, Sia planned to travel back to visit Arley for a few days before the new year. They hadn't seen each other since the Roscoe statue dedication, but not a day passed when they didn't text, video chat or share a playlist. They'd grown very close through pixels, despite the miles apart between them.

"Keep driving," Arley said, after she checked the time. "The ceremony starts in ten minutes! I'm going to change outfits back here. Don't look!"

"Change in the backseat? Is that safe, Arley?" her dad asked from the passenger side.

"Oh, our Arley knows what she's doing," her mom countered from behind the wheel. "Okay, dear. We won't look until you tell us you're ready. I want you to have privacy!"

Arley reached in her duffel bag and pulled out a black faux-leather jacket, a white flannel scarf and a black beret with silver threading. It added a celebratory accent that transformed her look from travel wear into wedding ready. Arley had a way of pulling off Gucci-level fashion on a corn nuts budget. As she slipped all the items over her black jumpsuit with its frayed-feather trim, she texted Sia to confirm something: *The ceremony is outside, right?*

Ding.

Sia: Even in this cold. My mom insisted they get married next to the statue...even if we all freeze before they say, "I do."

Arley checked her look using the camera on her phone and noticed the rainbow pin attached to her jacket lapel. In Texas, she wore it wherever she went. That wasn't her routine at home. As she felt the hard metal edges, she started to unfasten the clasp on the back, until the voice from the driver's seat asked another question.

"Doing okay back there? Don't worry too much about what you wear, honey. These are your friends. Really, they're more than friends. They're your chosen family. And family is happy to see you just as you are."

"Thanks, mom. I needed that," Arley smiled, as she adjusted the pin in place on her jacket. On this visit, she wasn't hiding anything.

"We're here," her mom announced. "Show time!"

Snow covered the sprawling grounds of the North Star campus, leaving not a single blade of grass untouched by the early winter glaze. Streetlamps illuminated with flickering orange bulbs lit early for the mid-afternoon ceremony. Arley's mom turned the car down the main driveway and followed a trail of magnolia blossoms strung together by ivy, which guided guests directly to the altar. Emma and Charles' closest friends sat in rows of folding chairs perched in the snow. What began as a "small commitment ceremony" ballooned to a guest list that topped one hundred people. Even the arctic blast couldn't stop folks from coming to this event. Some were taking bets on whether Emma would show, but Charles wasn't worried. Guests huddled under blankets as they waited for Emma to walk down the aisle.

"Leave your bags, Arley," said her mom. "I'll get them home for you. Just enjoy this special day!"

Arley closed the backseat door and stood face-to-face with her reflection in the car window. She pulled her hair behind her ear and examined the woman in the glass. For the first time in her young life, she felt connected to the person staring back at her. With a smile on her face, Arley darted toward the ceremony. The snow under her black leather boots crackled like the fine sugar coating on a petit four as she rushed down the magnolia and ivy lined sidewalk. She scanned the crowd for a place to sit—chair after chair was filled, except for one in the very back.

Ding.

Emma: I see you made it! We were waiting for you. Let's get this show on the road!

Immediately, a violinist started the wedding march. Arley looked around, unable to find Emma anywhere, but she spotted Sia who waved from the front row and mouthed "Sit here!" Arley slowly crept along the inside of the aisle, hunched over in an attempt not to cause too much of a disruption. The wedding march grew louder as Arley took her seat next to Sia and exchanged big smiles with Patty and Bell.

"My people!" Arley said, then whispered, "but where's J.D.?"

"Oh, you'll see!" Bell promised. "You know he always has a surprise!"

In that moment, an acoustic guitar joined the symphony, and the crowd stood to discover Emma beaming from the end of the aisle, draped in a white coat as brilliant as the snow. It was her "something new," and it framed a stunning sapphire pendant which she had designed herself as her "something blue." Emma winked at Arley and blew a kiss at Sia as she passed her cheering section and stopped beside Charles at the altar.

"He cleans up good!" Patty whispered.

Charles' eyes swelled as he knelt down to place a bed of magnolia petals on the ground. He ensured she'd have a soft place to land after she walked through the slippery snow. As the music faded, Arley heard a familiar voice welcome the crowd over a loudspeaker. Standing at the altar between the bronze statue of Roscoe the dog and Trooper the mustang was J.D. the officiant.

"I welcome you all to this sacred space with our sacred friends, to perform a ceremony that is anything but ordinary. I can say the same for Emma and Charles. The couple met years ago on Langston Road when they united to save a little abandoned dog named Poppy. In fact, they were also saving all of us, in a way, by creating community. And, as we can see, they also created love. But I'll say it again, this is no ordinary love. This is...them. For this commitment ceremony, they have chosen to share their own vows in their own way. I should point out that Emma asked me to stress that despite the non-traditional ceremony, this is a legal wedding, and their tax break applies to this fiscal year. With that, I'll hand things over to her."

Emma nervously grabbed the mic from J.D.'s hand.

"Hello everybody! Welcome to our commitment ceremony," she said, holding the mic like she was about to do a standup comedy act. "Heck let's just call it what it is. This is a wedding, okay? It's a wedding. You got me!"

Charles smiled as he held onto her hand, his body exactly one step behind her.

"I want you all to know that I'm here today because, first, I need a new name." She looked at J.D. as she said "Professor Hodges has a nice ring to it, doesn't it? Y'all can register for my next class in the Spring! But I'm mostly here for another reason."

Her smile turned serious as she looked at Charles like he was the only person in the snowy field.

"I'm really here because I'm a dream chaser. I have been all my life. And all my life I did that on my own," she turned back to the crowd. "Big mistake."

"Huge!" Sia called out at her mother, as everyone laughed.

"All that changed after I met Charles. I learned something I want to share with all of you today: the most important part of life isn't the dream—it's who you chase it with. And Charles, that's you. It's always been you. It always will be you."

As one hand grasped the mic, her other hand reached out to touch his cheek. She whispered "And because of that I do. Ten times over, with you...I do."

Patty began to sob. Bell and J.D. smiled knowingly at each other. Arley, her heart racing, nervously grabbed Sia's hand for the first time since they started texting in the fall. She felt a soft squeeze back.

"Top that, Charles!" Emma laughed, as she passed the mic over to him and hugged her soon-to-be husband. With a smile on his face, he said nothing at all. Instead, he slowly stepped through the crunchy snow toward the Roscoe statue. No one had noticed the gemstone covered collar wrapped around the bronze dog's neck. He unfastened it, the same collar Emma made for Roscoe to offer health, love, patience, and happiness. Now, the blessing was for his bride.

"Something borrowed!" Charles announced, as he held up the collar.

Attached to the front, beneath the silver plate engraved "Roscoe," were two dangling wedding rings.

"With this ring," he said as he slipped a platinum band on Emma's finger, "I promise to be your person. For always."

Emma gazed back as she slipped a matching band on Charles' finger.

"For always," she whispered.

There in the snow, Charles and Emma's partnership expanded yet again. Like sharing a box of lemon head candies, they'd journeyed through the sour and arrived in the sweet. From strangers to friends to business partners to spouses...to forever.

Despite the snow, maybe even because of it, the wedding guests danced and ate and celebrated inside a heated tent well into the evening. The festivities flowed on until Emma and Charles drove away, a "Just Married" sign on the hood and empty dog food cans tied to the bumper, rattling down the highway making a joyously loud noise. As J.D. watched the taillights fade, he whispered to Bell.

"It's amazing, isn't it?"

"What's that, J.D.?"

"It's amazing how anything can happen in this life if we rely on one another."

Most everyone made their way to their warm cars except for the party hosts, Bell, and J.D., who joined Arley and Sia at one of the tables. They still had a lot of catching up to do. Everyone had so many questions about Arley's life in Texas, but Arley had just one question for J.D.

"Do you ever think about getting another dog?"

Bell smiled, leaning in eagerly to hear J.D.'s response.

"Well, funny you asked about that. There's something I'd like you to see," he said. "Do you have time to come to my office?"

She and Sia walked down the long hallway with plaques and photographs on the wall, plus several framed newspaper articles about the old black Lab made famous by the bronze statue. As she neared his office, Arley felt nervous about how she'd feel seeing the empty space where Roscoe used to sleep. It was her first time back since he'd died, and she felt a void grow in her chest. As she approached J'D.'s desk, she was distracted by a faint whimper from the other side of the wooden drawers.

"What is that?" Arley asked.

"I think you mean, *who* is that?" Sia replied.

There on the floor, curled up inside a corduroy dog bed, was a tiny black Lab puppy.

"I found him today," J.D. said. "He was by the statue when we were setting up for the wedding."

"My mom calls him Roscoe Junior!" Sia shouted.

J.D. lifted the puppy in his arms and gently petted it between its eyes, instantly soothing the canine's stress from meeting new humans.

"We didn't want to make a big scene out of it before the wedding but, it's so cold outside, I had to bring him in for the night." J.D. explained.

"Are you going to keep him?" Arley asked.

"Maybe," he said. "If no owner turns up."

"If they do, you should keep him anyway. Who could lose their puppy in a snowstorm?" Arley said.

"We'll do what's right," he said, "It sure looks like a young Roscoe, doesn't it?"

"Roscoe Junior!" she replied. "You have to keep him."

Throughout the rest of the snowy night, the little black pup slept peacefully in J.D.'s office. It did the next night, too. And the next. It stayed a week after the snow melted. And the weekend after that. But not on Christmas Eve, when J.D. decided it wasn't right for a puppy to grow up in an office. He brought the dog home to Bell, wrapped in a red velvet cloth that could have been from Santa himself. A small square tag dangled off the fringe with two words handwritten: *"To Us, From Roscoe."*

The End.

A MESSAGE FROM THE AUTHOR

Thank you for reading my second novel. If you enjoyed spending time *Between the Mountains*, please share a copy with a fellow dog lover or leave a review to help others discover how one dog can unite an entire community. Also, I'd like to invite you to Langston Road for the prequel, *Between the Causeways*. You'll learn how Emma, Charles, and Bell first met while trying to rescue a stray. In the process, they saved themselves. Order your copy now at www.JeremyCampbell.online or ask for it wherever books are sold.

Special thanks to Rachel Knowles, Amy Westmoreland, Betty Esslinger, Martha Pendley, Angie Hodges, Heather Stark, Frances, the First Monday Rock Man, Lori Laney, my husband Michael Klimis, Carole Campbell, and David Campbell. Also, thank you to the great dogs of my life: Taco, Bunky, FloJo, Junior, Willie, Blue, Bandy, Jake, Elwood, Gretchen, Skye, Bo, Rayna, Tobias, BayLeigh & Bootsie. Plus, a shout out to canine queens Charlotte and Abbey.

ABOUT THE AUTHOR

A true dog story in his small, Southern hometown inspired Jeremy Campbell to write his debut novel, *Between the Causeways*. His books focus on fictional worlds inspired by actual events and the best of humanity. As an award-winning television journalist based in New York City, Campbell's storytelling career has taken him from the coast of California to the source of the Nile River. Years of covering news events has also contributed to a recurring theme in his writing: sometimes the worst things to ever happen lead to the best.

To book speaking engagements, visit www.JeremyCampbell.online or contact thelangstonpress@gmail.com.

An excerpt from...

295

Between the Causeways

Inspired by a True Dog Story

Jeremy Campbell

The Langston Press

New York City

This novel is a work of fiction. The names, characters and incidents portrayed in it are the work of the author's imagination. Any resemblance to actual persons, living or dead, events or localities is entirely coincidental.

ISBN 979-8-9866457-0-4 *(paperback)*

ISBN 979-8-9866457-1-1 *(hardcover)*

E-book also available exclusively on Kindle

For more information on this book and other works by the author visit www.JeremyCampbell.online

For Mama

*Sometimes the worst things to
ever happen can lead to the best.*

CHAPTER 1

Bell

April is the beginning of birthday cake season for Bell. Every week or so comes another reason to celebrate, always with cake. Two of them, to be exact. The first cake is the main event: a double vanilla masterpiece. A braided band of buttercream rounds the edges with blue flowers flourishing over the entire right corner of the cake. That's the section reserved for the first taste by the birthday girl...or woman.

Happiness tastes like a birthday cake to Bell. These divine delicacies must have marked one hundred special occasions over the years—always on her birthday, on her husband's birthday and on their anniversary, of course. Sometimes, she'll order a cake for "Gotcha Day." It's a holiday Bell rings in four times a year to celebrate the date she adopted each of her four dogs. When life begs for a celebration, the cake makes a cameo.

Waiting until after dinner to cut in to the creamy buttercream always feels like torture. That's where the second cake rises to the occasion. It's much smaller, but identical. Same round edges. Same braided frosting. Same blue flowers. Always. No one waits until after dinner to cut the second cake. That's the rule. If it's your birthday, you get to eat the second cake for breakfast if you want. Or sometimes the night before. Bell believes good things come to those who cake.

April is the beginning of birthday cake season for Bell, but what she couldn't see yet is that this year it also marked a new start for her. Once the winds of change blew through her small Southern town, no routine, hope or fear would be spared. So much waited ahead of her. However, on her drive home, Bell's focus was on the birthday cakes carefully secured in white paperboard boxes against the backseat of her SUV. She kept her eyes on both the "official" and "baby" cakes she got from the bakeshop on the town square for young Anna's special birthday celebration she was hosting. Bell's children are all of the four-legged variety, unless you count the thousands of second graders she taught before retiring last year. As a newly turned six-year-old, Anna was too young to be in Bell's class before retirement. Instead, her distinction is being among Bell's chosen family. That earns her two birthday cakes every year.

Flash. Flash. Flash.

From the driver's seat of Bell's SUV curving down Langston Road, the sun cut through the tall pine trees like a strobe light. It was hypnotic as she went over her to-do list.

Flash. Flash. Flash.

For a fraction of a second, each of the tall trunks of the pines blocked the bright beams shining from the other side of the trees lining the two-lane road. The rapid contrast of dark to light flickered like someone switching the lights on and off in the middle of an afternoon drive.

Bell took her usual way back alongside a thin strip of forest by the riverbank. The land is mostly untouched, other than an occasional pop-up campsite. Langston Road winds and curves for seven miles, like an asphalt line tracing the foothill of a mountain ridge. For most drivers, the dense green trees and the sparkling blue water more than make up for the slower speed required to navigate this scenic route. For Bell, it's the ride home.

Flash! Flash! Flash!

As she passed over the first narrow causeway, one of just two stretches of the drive not lined by a forest of trees, light beams reflecting off the water on each side of her exploded like a mirror ball. That's when Bell first noticed something unusual up ahead, positioned low to the ground on the roadside. She slowed down to take a closer look when something else caught her attention from behind.

Honk. Honk. Honk.

In her rearview mirror, Bell saw the familiar Jeep racing toward her. Each time she shares the road with this recurring motorist, the mysterious driver seems to pound her hand on the horn and slam her foot on the gas. Bell refers to the driver as the Jeep Lady. All she knows about her is that she zooms up from behind and rides too close to the bumper. It's a dangerous game on this curvy double-line road. Although Bell has never met her, she worries the Jeep Lady is going to cause a wreck one day.

Honk! Honk! Honk!

Bell swerved toward the side of the road, giving the Jeep Lady more room to pass, slowing down as the rock-covered roadside rumbled beneath her SUV. It was a bumpy ride—and the cakes! As soon as the Jeep rushed by, Bell pulled over by a strip of grass near the public boat docks and checked to see if the cakes slid across the back seat. There could be no cake catastrophe today.

She stood by the side of the road, her small frame appeared even more petite beneath the tall trees beside her. Bell opened the white cardboard boxes, confirming both cakes remained intact. As the sugary, freshly baked scent wafted toward her when the box opened, Bell privately wished they had slid enough to justify a light push to reposition them. If her finger happened to collect enough icing for a taste, it would be the Jeep Lady's fault. But, alas, both cakes were fine.

When she turned around to get back in the car, something was staring at her from the bushes. Whatever she'd seen on the edge of the roadway before caught up with her. Bell felt that unmistakable feeling that curious eyes were staring, and she vaguely made out the outline of something in the shrubs between all the pine trees. She stood still, thinking about the reports of bears and bobcats in this area.

"What is it they say to do..." she asked herself, "Run? Throw something? Stand up to make yourself as big as possible and scream? Or is that what you're not supposed to do?" Bell did none of these things. Instead, she called out to the creature.

"Hello? I'm friendly!"

The air hung still and quiet below the tall trees. The eyes that had been peeking through from a distance were gone now. Could Bell be seeing things? She took a slow step toward the driver's seat, giving it one more shot.

"It's okay if you want to come out to say hello!"

Still nothing, but Bell felt she was being watched.

As she drove off, she glanced in her rearview mirror, hoping to see what—or who—had been lurking along the road. Had she stayed a little longer, Bell may have gotten her first look at what would change her life and the lives of so many people whom she had yet to meet.

CHAPTER 2

The Cake Disaster

"Did you ever kind of feel like you've got to leave...and then you sort of feel like you've got to stay?"

The line from a song swirled in Bell's mind all day, thinking of her eldest dog. Time to go, time to stay. Bell wanted both for her eldest dog. Even in the rush to complete chores before the birthday party guests arrive, Bell's thoughts kept floating back to Skye's latest lab report from the vet clinic. Her old girl's test results showed data proving what Bell already expected—that her body had weakened and her pain likely had increased. The stoic canine would never allow signs to show that her back legs ache or that she struggled to catch her breath. She's the alpha dog, after all—she endures.

As Bell stared into her favorite pet's blue eyes, so bright the sky itself inspired Skye's name, a feeling rushed over her that maybe it was time for her beloved dog to go, but Bell sure wanted her to stay. At fourteen, Skye had lived a full life by the lake with her three canine siblings…and Chester, the world's most annoying parrot.

Chirp. Chirp. Chirp.

His squawking voice momentarily distracted Bell from her melancholy. Her husband J.D. describes the sound of the bird's voice as "a beautiful reed instrument." It's a biased opinion, as most guests hear the sound as a shriek echoing within the high ceilings of their living room. Whenever the green and white parrot chirps, Bell assumes he wants to perch on her hand. As his coarse feet wrap around her index finger, Bell's childhood dream of living in harmony with animals, just like Snow White, comes alive. Then reality always kills the fantasy, as the bird blatantly flaps his wings and takes a bite out of his keeper. Despite all his rage, the pinch of his beak never breaks the skin. The distasteful routine is the most definitive "Chester move" the devilish bird regularly plays on Bell, and she always falls for it. No matter their temperament, Bell cannot resist loving her pets. Her devotion to them is admired by J.D.

They met as teenagers. Bell was a quiet cheerleader more comfortable at home than in front of a crowd. The team's studious quarterback with horn-rimmed glasses asked her for dance lessons. Fifty years later and they're still spinning in circles together. Same shy smile, but J.D. wears contacts now, not glasses. When he was named director of the local community center, he launched a free monthly dance class, hoping it may connect a new generation with their future love. J.D.'s as dedicated to helping people as Bell is to helping pets. Between the two of them, no stray—with paws or the two-legged variety—walks alone.

Squawk. Squawk. Squawk.

Chester voiced his disapproval when the other dogs burst into the house after their day of roaming through tall, marshy hay pastures surrounding the lake on the farm. They have a routine, too. The young canines shake off the moisture, roll in the grass, then run in the house through the doggy door to join their elder sister Skye, who mostly stays inside to escape the heat.

As pack leader, Skye is the most respected of the pack. She was the first to arrive at Bell and J.D.'s home on the lake. Bell was driving home fourteen years ago when a metallic gray trash bag caught her eye. It was blowing erratically along the roadside, appearing almost as though something was rolling around inside it. Turns out, something was...Skye! Someone abandoned her as a weeks-old puppy, hidden inside a trash bag and left for dead along Langston Road.

As J.D. puts it, "There's a special place in hell for that kind of person."

For Bell, the trash bag may as well have been a gift sack decorated with bows and ribbons. She instantly fell in love with the pup, who had fur as white as daisies and eyes blue like a technicolor sky. At that moment, Skye's pitiful puppy days were done. Bell and J.D.'s home, with sweeping fields to roam and a tranquil lake to wade in, became Skye's doggy paradise. She began as the youngest of three dogs but climbed in the ranks over the years. The atrocity of time is that it ticks faster for a dog, living a full life in a fraction of the years awarded to most humans.

"If there's a Heaven, I hope Skye's welcomed by Willie and Gretchen and Jake and Elwood and Blue and Bandy," Bell always says, naming her beloved pets now buried near the hill in the backyard.

There hasn't been a single day in the past three decades that Bell and J.D. haven't woken up with a dog waiting to be fed, petted and loved. In recent years, the pack grew to three, four and then the bird flew into the mix to make a menagerie. With Skye's dwindling health, they fear their roll call will soon be down to only three dogs. As the line from the song in her mind says, Bell very much wants her to stay, but also hopes Skye will go without suffering when the time is right. But not on birthday cake day.

Time may beat quickly for Skye now, but her pace remains slow. As Bell laid out the napkins and silverware for the cake cutting, Skye stood smiling and wagging her tail. Those bright blue eyes said more than words ever could. The sunlight beamed through the picture windows in the living room, igniting her white fur in a yellow glow as she hobbled back to her doggy bed. She remains regal, even if her body can't keep up with her spirit.

By 11 a.m. both of the cakes sat ready for the party, ready for Anna to arrive. Streamers hung over the banisters of the stairs and two balloons danced in the corner of the ceiling. Everything was ready, and for the first moment of the day Bell sat down to catch her breath from preparing for guests all day. She shut her eyes to rest as a large white and gray paw plopped in her lap right on top of her hand.

"BayLeigh, do you want to hold hands, girl?" Bell smiled.

The nine-month-old sheepadoodle stared up at her mama, paw to hand, then looked over at the door.

"Do you need to go outside?"

Bell realized maybe, just maybe, the house training was working. She jumped up and led BayLeigh to the French doors that open to their backyard. The sheepadoodle trotted by her side, prancing straight out into the grass before bolting away to chase a pair of geese that waddled by the lake about a hundred yards away. She watched

BayLeigh in the sunlight, running and leaping and rolling in the fresh grass. They'd never had a pet quite like her before—so poised, smart and mischievous. After a few more laps, BayLeigh pawed on the glass to the front door, and Bell let her in.

"Good girl! Did you...do your business?" Bell asked, expecting to relish in the progress of her housebroken pup. But BayLeigh walked right past Bell and did her business on the puppy pad left in the corner of the living room.

"Oh, BayLeigh! You're the only dog who asks to be let inside to go to the bathroom!"

"They're almost here!" J.D. yelled down to Bell.

She heard the dogs barking, like they always do, when someone turns the corner onto their long driveway. Their warning gave Bell just enough time to quickly brush her short blonde hair and smooth her hands across her blouse to brush off any dog fur. Nestled between a lake and a mountain ridge, acres of fields and farmland surround their home. For the couple's thirty years there, they've enjoyed a front-row seat to the spectacular live show nature offers, from the ripples of jumping fish to spotting a king snake slithering across the drive to watching a heron that's made its large nest in a tree in their cove.

Bell loves her home. Whenever she looks out her kitchen window, it feels like she's watching a

National Geographic documentary in real time. Every spring, she counts ducks and Canadian Geese as they hatch around the lake and grow up to venture out into the world. Some of them stick around and receive names. More than the connection to nature, Bell loves that the property offers a safe space for her dog family to roam free. On hot summer days, her twin retrievers wade in the lake while her sheepadoodle playfully chases the sneaky beaver that gnaws on trees around the yard in the middle of the night. The family's blue-eyed canine matriarch knows that standing beside the bench at the tip of the property is the spot where a guest is most likely to sneak her a bite of a cheeseburger during one of Bell and J.D.'s cookouts.

Their small, one-lane driveway winds through the fields of hay and grass. It connects to Langston Road, the main route in and out of their small town. Their dogs, with sharp canine senses, always bark the moment a car turns from Langston Road onto the gravel drive leading to the lake house. Usually, Bell and J.D. have about ninety seconds from the first bark until the guest's arrival outside their home.

"Let's wrangle up the dogs so they don't scare Anna," J.D. suggested.

"I'm wrangling up poo-paws right now, J.D." Bell said.

"Poo-paws" are what Bell discreetly called the trail of evidence BayLeigh left behind revealing that the sheepadoodle's housebreaking lessons remain incomplete. In fact, the dog left drops of this unsightly evidence scattered across the living room floor. Bell cleaned and disinfected the area as she heard her dog family on full alert.

Bark. Bark. Bark.

Skye, with a slobbery, wide-eyed grin on her face, stood in the grass by the road. Her tail wagged and face smiled, always excited for visitors. Her body may be too tired to run with the pack, but that tail flopped up and down anyway. Even in old age, she loved company. The twin golden retrievers ran in circles, unable to contain their excitement or figure out where to wait while those ninety seconds passed before they could greet Anna and her grandmother, Patty. Anna wasn't sure about all those rambunctious canines. After all, at her age, they outnumbered and outsized her. Bell tried to herd the dogs away from her young guest.

"Dogs!! Come in! I have a treat for you!"

She tried to lure them into the garage, where she'd built the palace of all dog palaces for her canine family with beds, automatic feeders and air conditioning. However, with the van barreling down the last stretch of the farm road, the chance of containing their excitement, even with a treat, was not happening.

Honk. Honk. Honk.

"BayLeigh, stop that! Come in!! Come inside!"

It's always chaos when someone arrives in the driveway. BayLeigh, the youngest of the pack, cornered Patty's van, now parked outside. Still a puppy, she's already the largest of the dogs and by far the most energetic. Her poised poodle genes give her confidence and independence. Her sheepdog genes give her energy, joy and stubbornness. The sheepadoodle combination makes BayLeigh adored by everyone, no matter what trouble she finds. A swirl of canines surrounded Anna and her grandmother. That was not a problem for Patty, who barreled out of the driver's seat, practically lifting Anna to scoot her out of the passenger seat.

"Don't worry, Anna. These dogs are your friends," Patty insisted.

In an instant, BayLeigh darted past Anna, startling her enough for the child to spin around in a complete circle. BayLeigh galloped around Bell and wiggled through J.D.'s attempt to wrangle her before she leapt her way inside the house.

"That dog is faster than a hiccup," J.D. said, as Anna ran toward him with a hug.

"Happy birthday, Anna!" Bell smiled. "You slept for just one night, but woke up a whole year older! How does it feel being six?"

She didn't answer.

"Anna, it may feel even better if you have some cake," Patty said. "I heard Bell got you two of them! A big one for all of us to share, and another one just for you."

"They are in the kitchen. Go look!" Bell said, holding off the twin retrievers, who were still running circles around the guests.

Patty is more than a friend to them—she's the family you weren't born with, but are born to find. She's dependable, funny, and real in that tell-it-like-it-is way that makes you blush at first, until you laugh until you cry. She and J.D. met as coworkers at the community center J.D. manages in Skyline. Together they helped turn many dreams into reality for people in the small mountain town. As the years passed Patty became more like a chosen sister to Bell and J.D. That makes Anna a chosen granddaughter.

"You two spoil her," Patty said as Anna darted into the house for a peek at her cakes.

Bark. Bark. Bark.

"You two spoil her...and I love you for that," Patty added as she squatted down to wrap one arm around both retrievers. The affection seemed to soothe them, but it would be a short-lived silence.

Crash. Squawk! Crack. Bark!

"Ahhhhh!! AHHHHH!!! What did you do?!?" Anna's youthful voice pierced through the front door, sending the adults running inside.

"No! No, no, no, no! Stop it!" she screamed. "Bad!"

Anna's voice crescendoed to a pitch higher and higher, rivaling Chester's chirp. And rightfully so. She was absolutely covered in blue frosting with sprinkles of birdseed stuck to the buttercream smeared across the entire side of her face.

"That monster!" Anna locked eyes with Patty, whose look had a way of saying, *Take a deep breath before I take one for you* without speaking a syllable. Anna clenched her fists and tightened her lips into a pout.

"Oh no, Anna! Your cakes!" Bell felt heartbroken for the birthday girl.

"It wasn't me!" Anna explained, "It was...that...monster! Your dog needs to..."

She struggled to speak her mind without saying something she'd regret.

"It needs to go outside...and...chase a butterfly!"

Anna's angry tone turned soft as Patty raised her eyebrows. She turned around quickly, hands clasped to her chest with her back to BayLeigh, who was furiously licking the cake up off the kitchen floor. Patty burst out in laughter.

"Baby girl," Patty said, "How on earth did you get an entire cake's worth of icing...on your rump!"

Anna looked over her shoulder and down at her frosted backside as BayLeigh ran up and took a taste. The six-year-old's outrage showed in her squinted eyes and hands clenched tightly at her waist.

"That dog can kiss my butt!"

"Well, she looks like she is enjoying that!" Patty shot back, unfazed by her granddaughter's sass. "Let's get you cleaned up!"

And with that, Anna flashed her signature smile. "I am pretty sweet, aren't I? No wonder the dog wants a taste!"

Patty lifted Anna up to the kitchen sink to rinse away the icing and birdseed. Bell escorted BayLeigh outside through the doggy door and re-caged Chester, as the parrot flapped its wings in angry protest. In the half an hour it took to get things back in order, they made sense of what had caused this mess. BayLeigh seemed to have burst into the kitchen, raced Anna to the cake table and leapt up toward the counter. In one swoop, the sheepadoodle took a giant bite from the second "baby cake" while pawing the large one down to the floor. Anna dodged the falling desert so fervently that she bumped Chester's cage, spilling birdseed and opening the door enough for him to fly just a few feet, landing near the birthday cake massacre. From there, it's unclear who smeared the most icing—Anna, BayLeigh or Chester—as the trio of spirited creatures and child competed to block each other from the frosted delicacy. In the end, Anna landed seat-down on the larger cake.

It was a birthday cake disaster that will be told for years to come with belly laughs, but today Bell could only think about one thing: Anna doesn't have a birthday cake! All of her planning, her preparation and her hope that everything would be "just right" for Anna's birthday visit came crashing down. As hard as she tried to prepare for everything, life always has a way of thinking of something she missed.

"I'm so, so, sorry," she said—and she meant it.

"For what?" Patty exclaimed, "You gave me a story to tell Anna's prom date in about ten years. We'll be laughing about this one for a long time."

"I wanted everything to be perfect for you and Anna."

"Bell, this is perfect. Really, it's a great day!" Patty said.

"But...it's not what I planned. It's not the way it should be for Anna."

For weeks, Bell planned every aspect of this day, from the food to the decorations to the little surprises hidden around the house for Anna to discover. She even had the dogs bathed, so they'd smell fresh, like strawberries, after the groomer used Bell's favorite doggy shampoo. For days, Bell nervously watched the weather forecast fearing it might rain, which would make the yard muddy, the dogs stink, and ruin the view out the living room window. She wanted every detail to be perfect for this six-year-old's afternoon visit.

Thud. Thud. Thud.

Anna ran back into the living room.

"You like my new dress?" Anna asked. It was more of a statement than a question.

Her dress was actually one of Bell's t-shirts. It hung down to Anna's ankles. In the center was a bright, smiling face of a golden retriever that looked a lot like Bell and J.D.'s twin goldens. Written in a circle around the face of the dog, the shirt read "Puppy Love Lasts Forever."

"I love it, Anna. That's my favorite shirt, well...dress," Bell played along. "And it's true, the love for your dog lasts forever and ever and ever."

"Now Anna, you should ask Bell before you go borrowing her best dresses," Patty said.

"Well, my big puppy ruined the dress you came here in, so I think we're more than even," Bell said.

They were already laughing about the ridiculousness of the wild frenzy. Patty's amusement lingered like a rainbow after the rain, making the sticky clean up worth it. However, Bell couldn't resign herself to a birthday with no cake. You don't just go without it on birthdays. In an instant, she created a plan. She would fix this all with a quick trip back to town.

While Patty and J.D. entertained Anna, Bell made the trek to pick up cupcakes from the bakery. As she crossed over the first causeway bridge, Bell approached the spot where she'd pulled over along Langston Road the day before. She saw a familiar foe. The Jeep Lady was parked in the same spot as Bell earlier that morning. Her face seemed distraught, as though she was in the middle of something upsetting. It was the first time Bell had ever seen her, other than the distorted view behind the tinted windows of her Jeep. The Jeep Lady seemed younger than Bell imagined. Her face appeared soft, nothing like her aggressive persona that ruled the road. But standing outside of her vehicle, the Jeep Lady's eyes revealed worry and stress.

Bell pulled over to ask if she needed help. The sound of Bell's car approaching must have diverted her. Before Bell had a chance to even step out of her SUV, the Jeep Lady hurried into her driver's seat and took off, kicking up gravel from the road shoulder as she did.

Normally, Bell would have kept driving. After all, this stretch of land between the two bridges on Langston Road was wild and uninhabited. However, the feeling that something was waiting in the woods for her lingered. Without getting out to explore, there was no way to know. So, she did.

"Hello! It's me again! Remember? I'm friendly."

As Bell called out to the forest, there was a slight shuffling sound in the distance.

"Come on out!" Bell yelled, as she thought she must be crazy.

A branch snapped from another direction this time. Bell was not alone and felt a bit frightened. Perhaps she was stumbling across one of those secrets hidden in the woods she'd heard about as a child. It can be beautifully dangerous between the river and mountain, and there are horror stories about what happens when you fall on the wrong side of the story.

"Don't become a statistic," she told herself as she snapped around quickly, turning her back to the woods as she prepared to return to her SUV. But as she did, she heard a whimpering sound coming from over her shoulder. Bell froze. The whimpering grew louder, closer. She was afraid to move a muscle. While most every instinct in her body told her she wanted to go, Bell's heart wanted to stay. It was racing. She couldn't shake the feeling something was calling to her as she took a deep breath and softly began to sing to help calm herself.

"I see green in the trees... the yellow daisies, too."

The rustling leaves sounded closer over her left shoulder. From over her right shoulder, she sensed soft footsteps, but the cadence felt off. They couldn't be from a human. Are they the steps of a bobcat? A bear? What sort of trap had she stepped into? She kept singing.

"I see them grow... beauty for me, beauty for you..."

Suddenly, Bell heard a sound she recognized all too well. She'd even heard it less than an hour ago when BayLeigh gobbled up Anna's cakes. It was the sound of an animal panting in the heat.

"And that's how I know... the world is beautiful for us."

One deep breath later, Bell turned around to face whatever was lurking behind her. There she stood, almost within arm's reach, with two scruffy wild dogs.

* * *

Find out how the story ends. *Between the Causeways* is available now at www.JeremyCampbell.online, or ask for it wherever books are sold.